A
Picture Perfect
Christmas

CANDEE FICK

DEDICATION

To all my faithful readers
who begged to know what happened next...
I listened.
And this book's for you.

PROLOGUE

Postmarked March 12

Dear Mrs. Foster,

I hope this letter finds you well and in a receptive-enough mood to allow me to introduce myself. My name is Ryan Callahan, and I'm in love with your daughter.

While I'm completely aware of your husband's decision and actions to disown her, I serve a God who is more than able to change hearts. He is the same God who brought Liz into my life and opened the doors for us to work together on assignment for Bricker Communications Group. In fact, by the time you read this, we'll be in Fiji, where we will spend several weeks photographing the landscape, culture, and people as part of a book project, before moving on to another island in the South Pacific.

Because of God's great love, I'm holding out hope that someday your family may be reunited. This is especially important since I have asked Liz to marry me. Which brings me back to my introduction, in hopes that you can get to know me a little and trust me to take care of your daughter.

I'll start at the beginning. I was born and raised in Montana...

* * *

Postmarked April 17

Dear Mrs. Foster,

It's me again, Ryan Callahan.

I hope you've received our previous letters, and I pray you'll be open to being pen pals of sorts once Liz and I return to the States. As I mentioned before, my home base is my sister's house in Fort Collins, so if you felt like replying, you could send a note to her address and we'll get it after our travels conclude. (I'd say you could text me, but cell service is unreliable where we are. Not to mention, international rates are expensive. Might as well stick to pen and paper for now.)

In the meantime, I thought you might enjoy an update on our latest assignment in Tahiti...

* * *

Postmarked May 25

Dear Angela,

(Addressing a letter this way feels awkward since we've never personally met, but thank you for requesting the informality.)

Liz and I are finally back in the States. Despite the jet lag, we were so excited to see your letters waiting at my sister's house. In fact, I never fully understood how tears could be happy until I witnessed Liz squealing and dancing around the room, clutching the trio of envelopes in her hands. For that alone, I thank you.

First off, we understand your desire to keep our correspondence a secret and are simply grateful for the opportunity to communicate. Liz is moving into her new apartment tomorrow, and I'll include the address below if you wish to write to her directly. I plan to continue camping out in my sister's guest room for another few months and can forward Liz's letters from this address.

Based on your letters, you received our previous updates about our island-hopping adventures—all except for the last stop in West Samoa, which was bittersweet. It is a gorgeous country with amazing people, and I hope our work captured the essence of the land.

While we thoroughly enjoyed the assignment and the opportunity to experience yet another culture (and for Liz to gain another stamp in her passport and a few more freckles across her adorable nose), I was also ready for it to be over. On one hand, we were both exhausted from the weeks of endless travel—along with craving good old American food. On the other hand, the time spent working together has truly bonded us both personally and professionally so it was hard knowing that our special time together was drawing to a close.

Our boss has given us a few weeks off to recover and for Liz to get settled into her new place. The vacation will also give us time to dream about the future and start making more permanent plans....

* * *

Dear Mom,

I'm so sorry to hear about Dad's heart scare, and I'm glad you were there at the studio to call for the ambulance. At least you caught the symptoms before they caused any lasting damage.

I can already imagine Dad grumbling about the doctor's orders to cut back on the ice cream and start exercising. Maybe he will take this chance to slow down a bit and fully recover his strength. Hopefully having him around the house more doesn't cause you any trouble.

I briefly considered making a quick trip back to Kansas, but I was afraid my sudden appearance might finish what the clogged artery didn't. If you feel like it won't add too much stress, please let him know I'm praying for him.

On a different note, Grant McHenry (our boss) is sending Ryan and I on an assignment to Argentina. Another stamp in my passport! And since it's in the Southern Hemisphere, I'm hoping for a bit of an escape from the midsummer heat here in Colorado.

Even after our big-city New York adventure in June, I'm still in the mood for experiencing places very different from where I grew up. However, once all that is behind us, we'll need to get serious about taking jobs closer to home. Especially since it's past time to start planning our wedding....

* * *

Postmarked August 17

Mom,

I can't believe you actually talked Dad into taking a real vacation. And all the way to Maine! It must have been quite a change for you Kansas-dwellers to see the ocean. I still remember my first views of Hawaii back in March. Was the fresh lobster as delicious as they say it is?

Please tell me Dad took along a camera and used it for something fun outside of work. If you can manage to sneak copies, I would love to see a few pictures from your trip, especially if you have one of the two of you. It's been so long since I've seen you, and part of me wants to actually "see" that Dad is doing better in his recovery.

Argentina was quite the change of pace…and weather. I was glad I packed warmer clothes, especially when we headed to higher elevations. But the people were so nice and welcoming and willing to be photographed, and I'm certain that, along with the stunning landscapes we were also able to capture, this book will be a quality addition to the overall series.

Of course, rumor has it that we'll be taking another trip after the first of the year to retrace our steps and show the seasonal changes once Argentina is in the height of their summer. Plus, we may be assigned a second country or two within the series, so there's even more semi-guaranteed income on the horizon.

For the first time, it felt like I was truly a professional on the job instead of an apprentice following Ryan's lead. He's shockingly talented but extremely humble.

And he's the most romantic man I've ever met. Even in the middle of our packed itinerary, he arranged a few private dinner dates to get us out of "work mode" and focus on our relationship for a couple of hours. I hope I can be the wife he deserves....

* * *

Postmarked September 28

Dear Mom and Dad,

Enclosed is an advanced reader's copy of *Exploring Fiji*, the first book in the Journey to the South Pacific series. I can honestly state that every picture you will see within the pages was taken by either Ryan or myself. It is scheduled to release in January, with the remaining four books in the series launching every other month thereafter.

When I first started taking pictures with Grandpa O'Neill, I never imagined I'd end up here....

* * *

Postmarked October 22

Mom,

Did you really say that you caught Dad peeking at the Fiji book on your coffee table? I know I'd be pressing my luck to ask what he thought of my pictures this time around, but that doesn't stop my curiosity.

I'm glad he's taken up a hobby, even if I can't imagine him wearing coveralls and cutting wood. Here's hoping he'll keep the sawdust out in the garage instead of tracking it through the house.

Different subject. How is he really handling Jerry's defection? I don't want to say I tried to warn Dad, but it doesn't really surprise me that the scumbag took the client database and most of the bank balance with him. However, I know Foster's Fotos will survive the transition. Dad's reputation in the community and his contacts at church have to be worth something, even if he won't sue his former partner for breach of contract. Assuming they even had a written contract.

Anyhow, let me know if you need anything. Even with wedding expenses, I've got plenty in the bank.

Speaking of weddings, I can't wait to become Mrs. Ryan Callahan. Working together on all those photo shoots gave us a lot of time to talk, and I know I'll soon be marrying my best friend. Not to mention, he loves to spoil me. You would not believe what he gave me for my birthday....

* * *

Postmarked November 8

With great pleasure,
Elizabeth Foster
and
Ryan Callahan
invite you to join them
at the celebration of their marriage
on Tuesday, December 27,
at five thirty in the evening.
Gateway Bible Church
Fort Collins, Colorado
Reception to follow at the
Fort Collins Senior Center.

CHAPTER ONE

Liz Foster collapsed against the couch cushions and buried her hot face in a decorative pillow. "I can't believe you just said that." At her former roommate's laugh, she peeked over the fringed edge long enough to catch the other woman's smirk and hurled her shield toward the other end of the couch.

Dani Sheridan dodged the flying fabric. "You're about to be a married woman, so someone needs to tell you the truth."

"But saying that all the kisses make up for the dirty underwear on the floor...?"

"And misfires around the toilet." Dani retrieved the pillow from the carpeted floor and hugged it to her chest. "Yes. It's true. Along with other nasty aromas like body odor, gas, and morning dragon breath. Marriage can be messy." Dani wrinkled her nose and then sighed with a dreamy smile. "But the benefits of doing life beside the man of your dreams make the journey worth every inconvenience."

"With your vast experience of five months—"

"Going on six—"

"Yes, how could I forget?" Liz rolled her eyes. "I was right beside you when you said your vows."

"Just like I'll be there for you in four and a half weeks."

"Which is the real reason I invited you over this morning." Thanks to the open floor plan, Liz easily eyed the clock over on the wall above the small dining-room table. Despite living in the same apartment complex, their schedules rarely allowed time to get together. "I know we both have family Thanksgiving dinners in a few hours, but I've got this awful feeling that I'm forgetting something."

Planning a wedding without her mother's help had been a challenge logistically. And emotionally.

"Let's see what you've got so far." Dani pointed at the binder on the coffee table beside their empty mugs. "I'll do my best to fill in the gaps."

"Thanks." Liz scooted closer to her matron of honor and picked up the only organizational tool that kept her somewhat sane as she juggled the myriad of details. She flipped to the master checklist sandwiched between a calendar page and a stack of printed invoices and contracts.

"Obviously, both the church and the reception hall are reserved, since we had to know that information to print the invitations. I've got my dress, with a final fitting scheduled for two weeks before the big day. And my shoes, tiara-inspired veil, and jewelry are already purchased and waiting in the closet of the guest bedroom."

Dani opened the calendar app on her phone. "The fitting is the same day we're scheduled to pick up the bridesmaids dresses, right?"

In addition to Ryan's sister and Dani, the other bridesmaids were two of their former theater housemates. The only housemate missing—the diva of the bunch—had moved out of state earlier in the summer, and they'd lost touch.

"True." Liz confirmed the date on her printed calendar. "And the guys are getting their tuxes measured earlier that week, so all the attendants are covered."

"Good. What about the ring bearer and the flower girl?"

"Ryan's niece and nephew are filling in as junior attendants, so their clothes are included with everyone else's." Liz scanned the squares filled with her scribbled notes. "We pick up the rings on Monday."

Dani twisted the diamond ring on her left hand. "Good. Then all you *really* need is a preacher and the wedding license."

"Right. The license." Liz paused to add a note to the checklist. "However, the pastor is already lined up, along with our premarriage counseling sessions. Plus, I've got a meeting scheduled with the church's wedding coordinator, which is when we'll pick the music." Liz skimmed over the pages in front of her.

Her mother would certainly have an opinion about the music for sure. If she wasn't a faceless, long-distance pen pal.

"So the next logical step is decorations."

Liz forced her attention back to Dani's words. "Since we picked a Tuesday evening for the wedding, to make it easy for our theater friends to attend"—Liz paused to wink at her best friend—"the sanctuary will still be decorated with lots of greenery, poinsettias, and white twinkle lights from the Christmas services, so all we need to add are the candelabras, the church's white runner, the arch, and our fresh flowers." She grinned. "And before you ask, I have a meeting with the florist on Wednesday."

"A Christmas-themed wedding will be gorgeous."

"It's perfect. Plus it's a magical time of year, especially for us." Once upon a time Liz had dreamed of a beautiful wedding to the man of her dreams. And just last year, God had used a romantic walk with Ryan in the snow after they'd been at a wedding to nudge her back toward church and her faith. What better time to celebrate the next chapter of her life than around the festive reminder of God's ultimate love story?

"Who's the photographer for your wedding?"

"Ryan called in a few favors from friends."

"Ah. So your groom is helping after all?" Dani pursed her lips.

Liz's face heated. "Actually, except for the awards banquet we photographed together a couple days ago, he's been handling most of our business contracts and leaving me free to organize the entire wedding. Well, everything but the photographer and the honeymoon."

While their arrangement gave Ryan a wealth of travel and creativity, it left her behind with a raging case of jealousy and bridezilla-inducing stress.

"You're not alone there. I planned most of our wedding by myself while Alex finished up his final semester of classes. But speaking of honeymoons, do you know where you're going?" Dani's attempt at waggling eyebrows nudged a smile back to Liz's face.

"Not yet. But I do know that in mid-January we're going back to Argentina, probably followed by another country or two. Those might be working trips, but—"

"You'll also have time to yourselves in exotic locations on the company's dime."

"Exactly." At times like this, she could hardly wait to have the event behind them so they could focus on building a lifetime of memories together. And recapture the joy of traveling and working together as a team.

Dani glanced at the calendar pages. "We've covered the church decorations, but what about the ones for the reception?"

For the next several minutes, their conversation centered on tablecloths, centerpieces, and a balloon arch. Liz continued making notes on her calendar and adding items to the various shopping lists as the talk moved on to the wedding cake and catering menu.

"I think that covers everything for the reception except getting a final head count to the caterer by their deadline." Liz circled that note on her calendar and added a star. "How much did you pad your RSVP count?"

"I think my caterer suggested five percent, but check your contract." Dani glanced at her watch. "I need to head out soon, but speaking of RSVPs, have you heard from your parents yet?"

Liz swallowed the mixture of anger and hurt threatening to surface. "No. I know the invitations only went out two weeks ago, but I had hoped to hear more than the sound of crickets by now. Still, I shouldn't be surprised." She sighed. "Even after all the hints I dropped to Mom, she's never asked me about the wedding or how I feel about Ryan."

While her income more than covered the expenses, weren't the bride's parents at least supposed to offer to help? Even if her parents' finances were tight after their business troubles, the silence served as just another reminder of her status as the disowned daughter.

Something months of letters had yet to change.

"I'm sorry."

"It's not your fault." Liz squeezed Dani's arm. "I have to keep reminding myself that our prayers are slowly being answered. Actually getting a response to my letters and then a gift card for my birthday—even though it was late—mean we're making progress in rebuilding our relationship."

Even if it wouldn't be completely restored in time for the wedding.

But speaking of the main event…

Liz slid her planning notebook back onto the coffee table. "Rather than focus on what I can't change, I'm trying to celebrate this season of love. And thanks to these lists, I should have enough to keep my mind and body occupied every day between now and Christmas. Even before I add the gift shopping, wrapping, baking—"

"Don't remind me." Dani groaned. "It's our first Christmas as a married couple and we're already having the live tree versus fake tree debate. But there's not much room in the budget for decorations anyway, so we may end up with a Charlie Brown special."

"I've seen your apartment. You've turned your one-bedroom unit into a home—but maybe you can pretend that your tree is the theater's onstage prop tree during this year's Christmas show."

Liz glanced around her living room. While her two-bedroom apartment wouldn't officially become *theirs* until after Christmas, she wanted to start creating more memories together. Perhaps she should ask Ryan to help put up a low-maintenance artificial tree in the corner near the fireplace. Or would it spark their own debate?

"I could try, but the whole family seems to be going all out this year to celebrate Karen's successful kidney transplant. And since today seems to kick off the holiday season and I still need to fix the traditional green-bean casserole...I'd better get moving." Dani snagged the purse near her feet and stood.

"Well, thanks so much for your help, and say hello to Alex for me." Liz walked her friend to the door, and after Dani snagged her coat from a hook, they parted with a hug.

After closing the door against the late November chill, Liz eyed the plastic bag of prebaked rolls sitting on the kitchen counter beside her wallet and camera case. At least her contribution for the dinner with Ryan's family didn't require any special culinary talent. Although now that John was home and healthy again, her future sister-in-law wanted to create new traditions. She had abandoned last year's menu of chili in favor of a roasted turkey with all the fixings.

Back then, Cheryl's Crock-Pot of chili had been the perfect ending to a perfect day of sledding with Ryan and his family—the day when their crash into a snowbank had sparked the beginnings of a romance.

The framed picture of Ryan and Liz with a lopsided snowman now graced her mantel as a reminder of last year's season of miracles. Starting with a nick-of-time job extension, she'd soon met Ryan, recaptured her love of photography, reaffirmed her faith in God, and been welcomed into Ryan's family.

Her eyes drifted to the photo of her parents standing by the ocean during their vacation to Maine.

Was it too much to hope for another miracle this Christmas? Because the only thing that would make her wedding more perfect would be walking down the aisle on her father's arm.

* * *

The difference a year made.

Ryan Callahan exited his truck and slammed the door before making his way across the parking lot toward his fiancée's apartment.

Soon to be *their* first home. Together.

Last year he'd arrived on the other side of the complex to pick up Liz for a day spent sledding with his family—a day powdered with fresh snow in the foothills and crystallized frost on the trees around Fort Collins. Just a week after they'd met, it was the first time he'd come close to kissing her laughing lips.

Today, although the temperatures hovered around forty degrees, there wasn't a snowflake in sight. Except in his memories.

They'd come a long way in the past year, but the sparks between them were still very real. Just a few more weeks and she'd truly be his. And he'd never have to leave her side again.

With long strides, he bounded up the flight of concrete-and-steel stairs and strode down the cement corridor. His knuckles barely grazed the metal surface before the door was yanked open.

Liz stood framed in the gap, a green sweater highlighting the color of her sparkling eyes above her wide smile. "You're right on time."

He pulled off his cowboy hat, stepped inside, and gathered the red-haired beauty into his arms. "Howdy, ma'am." After a quick kick to shut the door behind him, he lowered his lips to hers for a delicious kiss that held a hint of coffee. A flavor that shortly had him craving more, when her arms wound their way around his neck in response.

Reluctantly, he lifted his head and loosened the hold around her waist. Her eyes fluttered open, and although her hands slid off his shoulders, the banked heat of her gaze accelerated his pulse yet again.

But he'd do whatever he could to protect this woman, even from himself. After one last quick kiss, he stepped away. "I could get addicted to you, especially with such a warm welcome."

A cute blush spread across her cheeks. "I'll do my best to remember."

At least he wasn't the only one short of breath.

Needing to break the intensity of the moment, he shrugged out of his coat and hung it on a hook beside the door. After reaching into one of the pockets for Liz's gift, he turned back to face the woman of his dreams and handed her the small box wrapped in red paper and tied with a white ribbon.

"It's not Christmas yet." But the protest didn't stop her from accepting the present and clutching it over her heart.

He led her toward the couch with a smile. "No, but it is our one-year anniversary of sorts. And such a milestone deserves something special."

"As if your kisses weren't enough." A delightful blush coated her cheeks again. "Still, I suppose we'll be marking our relationship milestones by the holidays, making it less likely to forget them."

"Starting with Thanksgiving and the fact that I'm so thankful God brought you into my life." His eyes drifted across her face.

"And then Christmas, when I reconnected with God's love...and two days later will vow to love you forever."

He wrapped an arm around her shoulders and squeezed. "Don't forget about Valentine's Day and my Superman card." The day he'd known for certain he wanted her in his life permanently. And the day he'd taken the first step toward securing their working partnership.

"Valentine's Day." Her voice wobbled a bit.

Right. One of their first fights.

A simple misunderstanding on her part had almost doomed their future, until she'd taken one brave step with a gift of pudding cups to set him free to pursue his dreams.

Dreams which now included the two of them.

He pressed a kiss to her forehead. "We'll have to celebrate that day with chocolate pudding, even if we're out on assignment and have to pack it in our suitcases. But in the meantime, how about you open your present?"

Her brilliant smile returned, and a few moments later she'd torn through the paper, opened the box, and pulled out a six-inch-tall ceramic snowman ornament. "Oh, how adorable—and he almost looks like Herman, our snowman from last year."

"That's what I thought, but he's not the only thing in the box."

"There's more?" She pushed aside the rumpled tissue paper and found the envelope on the bottom. After opening the flap, she squealed. "I hoped we could see the new show."

He glanced at the tickets he'd bought last week, tickets to tomorrow night's opening of *The Miracle on 34th Street—The Musical.* "I'd thought we could make this a new Christmas tradition at the theater. This time without the hassle of cameras or printing and delivering pictures."

"Or costumes or dance steps, either." Liz winked. "I've always wondered what it would feel like to simply be a guest and enjoy the evening instead of worrying about my lines in the next scene."

"Well, I'm glad I'll have your undivided attention instead."

"Oh." Her eyes widened. "The second ticket is for you?" Her innocent expression dissolved with a wink. "There's no one I'd rather spend the evening with."

"Good." He dropped a quick kiss on her lips, then leaned back. "However, since we're supposed to be at John and Cheryl's soon, is there anything I can do to help you get ready?"

"Not really. I've got everything I need in a pile on the counter." Liz waved one hand toward the kitchen, then scooted to the edge of the cushions and stood. "Just let me find a home for this little guy and we can leave."

She crossed the room to the short bookshelf displaying a collection of framed pictures and small figurines from the various countries they'd visited together. He'd already discovered, when her souvenir shopping centered around T-shirts and tourist trap trinkets, that Liz treasured the moments and memories more than expensive gifts.

Not that he couldn't afford bigger purchases, like their rings and wedding expenses, but he was learning to speak his love in a language she would appreciate most.

Which was why the tiny snowman had caught his eye while shopping for a card.

However, instead of placing her newest gift on the bookshelf highlighting their travels, she moved on to the smaller display atop the mantel. To the space reserved for family moments.

As she arranged the miniature Herman beside the picture of them with the original version, he saw the photo of her parents.

How was Liz truly handling the wedding planning without her mother's input or presence? And what girl didn't dream of having her father walk her down the aisle?

It could be too emotional of a topic to open on their way to a happy gathering with his family. As they bundled back into their coats and made their way to his truck, he made a mental note to find out later.

Weddings were supposed to be a celebration of two families joining together. And while his parents wouldn't be present because they were both deceased, he still had his sister and her family.

Liz had no one to stand beside her except her pseudo-family from the theater.

And that broke his heart.

CHAPTER TWO

Liz inhaled the scent of roasting turkey the moment Ryan opened the door to his sister's house. "It smells like Thanksgiving in here." And the bittersweet memories of Christmases past.

Ryan's hand on her waist nudged her inside. "Maybe. But I'm still not sold on stuffing a bird with bits of bread."

"Spoken like a true Montana cowboy." One who'd told her stories of past holidays on their family's ranch being celebrated with slabs of beef instead of a silly bird.

They had barely cleared the threshold before a high-pitched yell warned of an incoming nephew: "Uncle Ryan's back!"

Liz managed to step aside to avoid the collision as Matt first launched himself at his uncle's waist and then tugged on his hand, dragging him back through the door they'd just entered. "Can we play catch?"

"Hold your horses." Ryan laughed. "I was only gone for an hour. Just give me a minute to get—"

"I'm glad you came, Auntie Liz." Hannah mirrored her brother's actions with a firm clasp around Liz's knees and an adoring gaze upward.

"Hi, precious." However, with the bag of rolls and a travel mug of coffee filling her hands, she couldn't even reach down to return the hug without risking the camera bag sliding off her shoulder and knocking the little girl over.

Cheryl's laughter echoed in the entryway as she approached from the kitchen. "All right, you two. Let go of them so we can at least shut the door and keep the heat inside."

After a few minutes of good-natured family chaos allowed her time—and space—to stow her camera bag and hang up her coat, Liz followed her future sister-in-law into the kitchen while the men promised to watch the kids.

"What can I do to help?" Liz found a small spot on the counter to set the bag of rolls and then eyed the array of pots and pans on the stove. At least the nearby table was already set.

"Check those potatoes to see if they're cooked enough to mash." Cheryl handed Liz a fork and then pointed from the largest pot on the stove to the mixer on the counter nearby. "Drain 'em and then whip 'em up with a big hunk of butter and a splash or two of milk. Meanwhile, I'll try to figure out how to make enough gravy from the turkey juices." She turned and began rummaging through a nearby drawer. "Beef is so much easier."

"If you say so." Liz poked the fork tines into a simmering potato and found a hard center. The next two she tried were the same. "At least you're in charge of the main dish, because I have no idea how to cook a turkey. My mom always started roasting it long before I got up."

"I wish I could say the same, but I found some great videos online with tips." Cheryl puffed out a breath as she eyed the small amount of amber liquid in the base of one pan. "I'm voting we go back to beef next year and forget that I ever came up with this dumb idea."

"Why don't you wait to see what the others think when they taste it?" Liz nudged Cheryl with an elbow. "Especially since you said John's family always had turkey when he was growing up. Hey, didn't he officially graduate from rehab this week?" While the doctors hadn't needed to amputate after the explosion overseas, John had suffered nerve damage in his legs, and it had taken months before he didn't need the assistance of a walker. Even now, he still occasionally used a cane for stability.

Cheryl nodded. "We have a lot to be thankful for, but I still don't want him to overdo."

While catching up on other family news, the two women somehow managed to not only dish up the food but also carve the turkey. Before long, they called the others and soon everyone gathered around the table.

Seated beside Ryan, Liz eyed the smiling faces of Ryan's family. Instead of focusing on what she could not change—namely her parents' choices—it was time to make new memories and focus on her future. A future with Ryan and this small family as her very own.

With those thoughts in mind, it was natural to join in as John prayed over their meal and thanked God for His many blessings on their lives.

Warm fingers grasped her hand and then squeezed. A moment later, her hand was lifted from her lap and a warm kiss pressed against the back of her fingers.

She opened her eyes and caught Ryan's gaze. The depth of love shining in his eyes brought tears to her own.

Soon and very soon.

"Break it up, you two." Cheryl's laughter and words echoed those from a year ago in the snowbank. Minus the snowball. "There are children present."

Across the table Matt gagged, but his smile gave him away. Especially when his father imitated Ryan's move on his own wife and Cheryl's laughter faded into a sappy sigh.

As they passed the food and loaded their plates, talk naturally turned to the upcoming wedding…and how soon Cheryl would get full access to her coffeepot again.

Ryan lifted his glass in an easy salute. "It won't be long until all the caffeine is yours." He waggled his eyebrows. "But in return, you lose your built-in babysitter."

"True. So we'd better use you while we can." John leaned closer to Ryan. "Can you watch the kids on Saturday night so I can take Cheryl to the movies?"

Ryan glanced at her with a raised eyebrow. "Liz?" He might be the official babysitter, but he'd want her right there beside him. Especially for a casual evening with chaperones.

"Sure." Liz grinned to let him know she liked his plan to spend even more time together.

John's laughter exploded around the table. "Good man— already checking with the real boss before you commit. As they say, happy wife…happy life."

Cheryl slapped her husband's arm, but that didn't stop her chuckle as she turned to help Hannah butter her roll.

"Seriously, though..." The tone in John's voice captured Liz's full attention as he eyed them both. "Married life isn't like the fairy tales starting with 'Once upon a time.' We've come through a rough season, and I've rediscovered the secret to a happy marriage. It's in being a servant. Put the other person's needs first, and you'll find your needs are met in return."

Something she'd already done when she left the theater behind. And God had blessed her abundantly in return.

God, thank You for all You've done for me. Help me to love and serve Ryan well as his wife.

Her eyes darted to her fiancé, only to find him watching her with a serious expression. His gaze captured hers, eloquently communicating a silent vow that preceded their spoken ones.

A delicious shiver ran up her spine. She could hardly wait to officially begin life with this man.

Around the table the conversation shifted once again, and despite Cheryl's earlier frustrations with the menu, the food quickly disappeared. Especially once they sliced into the pumpkin pie and topped it with freshly whipped cream.

"Can we do this every year?" Matt used a finger to swipe a bit of topping from his plate before popping it into his mouth.

"Use your fork, not your fingers." Cheryl pointed at his unused napkin. "And we'll see."

"My vote is with Matt." John nudged his wife. "The turkey was delicious."

"You might change your mind after a week—or two—of leftovers." Cheryl glanced from the half-empty platter of sliced meat to the half-carved carcass still in the roasting pan. "I'm going to have to research ways to use up all the extra turkey."

Liz laughed. "I think leftovers are supposed to be a part of the tradition—never-ending menus of turkey sandwiches and turkey potpie."

Beside her, Ryan shuddered. Did that mean she wouldn't have to cook any turkeys in their future?

"I suppose I could freeze some leftovers...and roast a smaller bird next time." Cheryl sighed. "However, I've got another new tradition for us to try."

John patted his stomach. "I hope it's not more food. I'm already stuffed." He winked at his kids. "Just like the turkey."

Cheryl rolled her eyes. "I wanted something we could do together as a family in the evenings between now and Christmas. Something to keep your father off his feet like the doctor said." She pretended to frown at her husband. "So I bought a ginormous puzzle and thought we could set up the card table in the corner of the living room."

"What a great idea." Happy memories from her childhood brought tears to Liz's eyes. "My family used to put together a puzzle every year when I was little."

"Like me?" Across the table, Hannah wiggled in her chair as if she couldn't wait to get started.

"Exactly like you. And even younger." Liz glanced at the others before focusing again on the small girl. "I used to sit on my dad's knee so I could see while we searched for the edge pieces."

Ryan squeezed her arm. Almost as if he knew how much she missed her parents and the happy family they'd been before Grandpa O'Neill died.

"Sounds like another great tradition for our family to adopt." John pushed back from the table. "Cheryl, the food was delicious. Now, why don't you ladies get out the puzzle and relax for a bit while Ryan and I clean up?"

"Please don't."

"What?" Liz glanced quickly between the couple and the pots and pans filling the sink.

Cheryl just shook her head. "I appreciate the thought, honey, but I really don't need to spend weeks trying to figure out where you stashed the clean dishes." She stood and motioned the kids toward the living room. "Liz and I can handle this mess while you and Ryan start the kids on the puzzle."

John rose to his feet with the help of his cane, then gave his wife a quick kiss. "Just remember, I offered."

She grinned. "Yes, and for that courtesy, I'll ignore the fact that you'll be watching the football game later instead of helping find the edge pieces."

John turned toward the door, but Liz didn't miss his wink at Ryan. "And that's how it's done...."

* * *

Friday night found Ryan seated at a small table for two on the second level of The Wardrobe Theater with a clear view of the stage. Every other table in the room was occupied with theatergoers, and the aisles were filled with wait staff carrying trays of covered plates.

Yet his eyes lingered on Liz as she spoke with yet another female cast member who had stopped by to chat about the wedding.

Perhaps he should have picked a different location for their date. Then again, Liz really wanted to see this show.

Their waitress—and Liz's best friend—Dani chose that moment to arrive with their meals.

"Scoot along." Dani hip-bumped the visitor and then sat a plate of prime rib in front of him. "These lovebirds are on a date."

The other dark-haired woman just laughed and leaned over to give Liz a hug. "We'll talk later."

Ryan breathed in the fragrant steam rising from the slightly pink meat and reached for his fork. "This looks delicious."

"It tastes good too." Dani winked as she delivered Liz's plate of chicken-something. "Anything else I can get for you two besides crowd control?" She glanced around the bustling auditorium.

"Maybe the inside scoop on the show? Any kissing scenes to inspire our own?" Ryan grinned across the table as a delightful blush covered Liz's cheeks.

"There are definitely a few kisses, but none for me. My offstage hero is the only one who gets to taste these lips now. Thankfully my father-in-law agrees."

Liz giggled. "Bet Alex gets a kiss before the curtain rises."

"Always." Dani squeezed Liz's shoulder, then moved on to serve the other diners in her section.

Despite the collective noise of chattering guests, Ryan lowered his voice for privacy. "Will I get a kiss before the curtain rises?"

Liz's gaze dipped to his lips. "I think it can be arranged." She turned her attention to her meal.

Thoughts of kisses—both onstage and off—made him extremely glad that Liz wasn't an actress anymore.

However, it was good to see Liz surrounded by her friends...the same friends who would be there in a few weeks to celebrate their wedding.

Now, more than ever, he wanted her to have the wedding of her dreams.

After a few bites of the juicy meat, he took a cue from his brother-in-law's Thanksgiving Day–cleanup offer and asked Liz whether there was anything else he could do to help with the wedding preparations. Then he braced himself as Liz unleashed the status of a long list of existing arrangements and the various appointments still to come. Apparently no detail would be overlooked until the outcome was perfect.

But at the end of the day, she would be his. What could be more perfect than that?

Even if his bride did seem more focused on the trappings than on their relationship, at least temporarily.

Then again, this was supposed to be a romantic date and not a working dinner.

Ryan swallowed the last of his prime rib, pushed aside his empty plate, and studied Liz until she blushed under his attention. But not before he noticed a glimpse of something else in her eyes. Something she tried to mask behind a wide smile.

Was it the cumulative stress from planning the wedding? Or exhaustion? Hopefully she wasn't getting cold feet.

Their plates had been cleared and the lights dimmed before he arrived at any conclusion.

After a quick kiss across the table, he settled back to enjoy the first half of the show—but his eyes kept drifting to his lovely fiancée. By the time the intermission arrived, along with a slice of pecan pie to share, it was obvious that Liz was not simply stressed.

Ryan took a deep breath for courage. "You seem a little sad tonight. What's really going on inside your pretty head?"

"Nothing." Her smile didn't quite reach her eyes.

He reached across the table to squeeze her hand and lowered his voice. "I love you, and I want to be here for you. Whatever you need. And even if I can't solve your problem—whatever it is—I still want to know how you feel."

Tears welled in her eyes as she finally waved a hand at the empty stage. "It's the mother-daughter scenes…. I'm missing my mom, especially this Christmas. After our letters, I guess part of me started hoping for a miracle in time for the wedding. And it's bugging me that—with only a month left—there's been no RSVP of any kind yet."

Yep. He'd been right yesterday when he saw the picture of her parents. And again when she'd mentioned working on puzzles with her dad. He shifted uncomfortably on his chair at the realization that he'd gotten wrapped up in the football game and never followed up on his instincts.

Liz might be putting a brave face on it now, but he still remembered holding her while she sobbed over the loss of relationship with her parents. Despite the progress they'd made, for them to ignore the invitation to her wedding had to feel like a fresh rejection. No wonder she was upset.

His heart broke for her ongoing pain. "I wish I could fix this for you."

Her smile wobbled a bit, but she squeezed his hand. "You're sweet, but only God can change their hearts."

"So we'll keep praying for them. And we'll try to be patient." If only they lived in a time of instant miracles…

She sighed. "I'm trying not to forget about the 'Reason for the season' in the middle of all the wedding plans. I need to keep my focus on God…and you…instead of on a silly party."

"Have I told you lately that I love you?" He stared into her eyes until a true smile ignited in their depths.

"You have. At least three times tonight."

"Only three? I must be getting rusty." He leaned across the table for a quick kiss, and then, with the reminder of his love hanging in the air between them, he turned his attention to the first part of her statement. "Maybe we can get an advent calendar to open and talk about together. It would help both of us keep our minds in the right place."

A slight smile curved her lips. "Like a new tradition for our lives together."

Before long, the lights dimmed again and the second half of the play distracted Liz from their conversation. If only it were that easy to forget the shadows in her eyes when she thought about her mom.

A nagging feeling gnawed at him inside. What if her mom hadn't been showing Liz's letters to her dad? What if the nonresponse to the wedding invitation was simply because she hadn't mentioned it yet? Was Liz's mom afraid of the reaction and just waiting for the right moment to bring it up?

Instead of worrying about her parents, his focus should be on his bride-to-be. Like John had jokingly said, a happy wife led to a happy life. And like Christ, he needed to put her needs above his own.

God, how can I serve Liz best?

In the quiet between scenes onstage, a whisper of an idea filtered into his heart. After mulling it over through several more scenes, he finally embraced the idea as the answer to his prayer.

He would extend the wedding invitation in person and pray that God prepared the way.

The play finally ended with the usual happily-ever-after kiss, this time in a fictional Macy's department-store window. While he waited beside Liz to greet the cast and celebrate the successful opening of an excellent show, Ryan launched the calendar app on his phone.

Between his photography obligations and the wedding appointments, it would be difficult to squeeze in a quick trip to Wichita. The upcoming week was packed full, but perhaps the week after would work.

That would give the Fosters another week to respond on their own before he intruded into their lives. And another week for him to pray for a favorable reception.

He slid the phone into his pocket and eyed Liz's carefree smile. While he hoped to bring the spark back into her eyes with a family reunion, he didn't want to get her hopes up.

Perhaps he should keep the true purpose of his trip a secret?

With Liz's mind so filled with wedding details, she might not even realize he'd been gone.

CHAPTER THREE

"I love how Christmassy the sanctuary looked this morning." Liz looped her hand into Ryan's bent elbow as he led them into their favorite restaurant. "Once we add our fresh flowers to the church's decorations, it's going to look stunning when I walk down the aisle."

Beside her, Ryan shrugged, but she caught the half smile on his lips.

"What? You don't like the decorations? Why didn't you say something when we met with the florist?"

He let the hostess know they needed a table for two, then turned to her with a full smile. "The wedding decorations don't really matter to me, since I'll only have eyes for you."

His off-key attempt to sing the final lyrics made her laugh. "Okay, you're off the hook." She punctuated her words with a quick kiss.

"How long until the wedding?" The college-aged hostess giggled.

Heat rose in Liz's face at the realization that they had an audience. "Just over three weeks now."

"Congratulations." The young woman gathered two menus. "If you'll follow me, your table is ready."

Minutes later, with their orders placed, Ryan reached across the table and grasped her fingers. "How did last week go for you?"

Over the past few months, they'd fallen into the routine of using Sunday afternoons to reflect on the past week and plan the week ahead. Beyond the logistics of their photography partnership, the weekly check-ins offered a level of accountability and often led to bursts of creative brainstorming for the business.

However, today, as she talked about all the wedding details she'd handled over the past six days, Ryan seemed distracted. Even if her gushing felt like trying to drink from a fire hose, he should at least pretend.

"Hey. You're not paying attention. Don't you even care?" *Yikes.* Where had that twinge of bridezilla voice come from?

"About what?" Ryan's eyebrows rose.

"Our wedding. What I've been talking about for the last fifteen minutes." She resisted the urge to roll her eyes.

"Of course I care about the wedding." He sighed. "But I guess I'm more interested in what comes afterward."

Liz blew out a frustrated breath. "Typical male, with his mind on the honeymoon."

New heat banked in his eyes, and she squirmed under the intense scrutiny. Probably shouldn't have brought up that particular topic.

"Now that you mention it, yes…but I'm also looking forward to a lifetime together. I asked about your past week because I care about *you.*" His gaze shifted from her lips to her eyes, and there she saw the truth of his words…and the depth of his love.

Her heart melted. To a guy, the color of the flowers might not matter, but Ryan had been trying to listen to her rambling because *she* mattered.

Before she could apologize for her high-maintenance moment, their food arrived. And their conversation shifted as Ryan wondered aloud whether a trip to photograph Italy—and experiencing the authentic flavors there—would ruin their appreciation for Italian restaurants in the United States.

Which made sense in a weird way, since she had a hard time eating tacos after visiting Argentina.

Once the debate had run its course, Ryan pulled out his phone. "So what's on your schedule for the coming week?"

She swiped into her calendar app. After seeing her to-do list, a wave of stress descended. "The theater girls are throwing me a bridal shower on Wednesday night. Even though we're still waiting on a final head count, I'm supposed to finalize the menu with the caterer. Plus I need to go shopping for the table favors." Not to mention the normal Christmas shopping, wrapping, and decorating. "What about you?"

"I have to shoot the wedding for Mrs. Stewart's nephew on Friday, and I need to meet with the couple in the morning to finalize the details."

Liz bit back her smile. Despite her past teasing and his protests, her fiancé sometimes donned the wedding-photographer role. In early November, she'd helped him at the wedding of mutual friends from their church. Friday's shoot was as a favor for his sister's next-door neighbor, since she'd been such a great backup babysitter while John had been deployed and later injured.

In the middle of her thoughts about past wedding shoots with Ryan, Liz almost missed his mention about heading out of town on Monday.

"Wait, that's not on my calendar." She quickly scrolled back through the dates.

"It just came up. I'll only be gone one night."

"I wish you would have told me sooner." She added the trip to her calendar. Right atop her rescheduled appointment with the caterer. Had she forgotten to let Ryan know of the change?

"Well, I told you now. Then when I get back, I'm filling in for the newspaper to cover Tuesday night's basketball game."

Right. Ryan handled their photography business by himself so she could focus on the wedding. And *that* business income paid the bills, even if it left her home alone with a detail-clouded mind when she'd much rather hop on a plane and further explore her creativity behind the camera.

She sighed. "I had hoped you would come with me to meet the caterer, but now you'll be gone."

He quirked the half smile that made her heart race. "You already know I love all kinds of food, and money is no object. Order a variety." His eyes dipped to her lips. "But know I'm saving you for dessert."

Her face flamed.

Liz was getting ready for bed before she realized she'd never asked anything more about his upcoming trip. Their conversation had bounced from kisses to gift ideas and back to the wedding itself but never returned to the work occupying Ryan's days.

Was she really so self-absorbed that she couldn't even bother to ask how *he* was doing? Especially after he'd listened to her wedding-obsessed monologue? She might have a one-track mind lately, but as John had said on Thanksgiving Day, she still needed to put Ryan's needs first.

God, please forgive me.

She laid her head on her pillow with a lighter heart...and a promise to call Ryan in the morning to find out more about the trip.

* * *

Monday afternoon found Ryan second-guessing his decision to fly to Kansas, especially when foggy weather delayed the flight. However, as he finally followed his phone's navigation instructions from the airport toward a neighborhood on the outskirts of Wichita, he had to trust that God had directed his steps.

Too soon, he pulled his rental car to a stop beside a modest two-story home on a block filled with similar residences. The bare trees and brown grass of winter seemed as bleak as the lingering fog and the absence of any cars in the driveway. He'd wonder if anyone was home, except a lamp glowed through the front window.

His earlier delays now put him in an awkward position. Instead of speaking to Liz's mother alone, Ryan now worried that her father could also be home from work. Or worse, would he arrive in the middle of their evening meal?

As he closed the navigation app on his phone, he caught a glimpse of Liz's face on the screen saver.

Liz.

The woman he loved second only to God.

And the woman he'd been dodging calls from all day, especially after her early text apologizing for not asking more about his trip. Not wanting her to worry—and not wanting to actually lie to her—he'd simply reminded her that he was busy with a wedding consultation and then traveling. She'd stopped texting only after he promised to tell her about the trip when he returned.

But in the meantime, he had to at least try to rebuild this bridge for her sake.

With a quick prayer for courage, Ryan shut the door on his rental car and strode up the sidewalk to the front door. As he approached, he caught the muffled sound of a television program playing inside. Hopefully it was a good sign that he wasn't interrupting their supper meal.

Before he lost courage, he knocked on the door.

A man's voice called out, and the volume of the television lowered.

With a churning stomach, Ryan fought to summon a respectful, professional expression on his face.

The door cracked open, and a plump middle-aged woman stared out at him. Despite her puzzled frown, he immediately recognized her from the picture above Liz's fireplace. But up close, though her red hair had streaks of gray in it, her resemblance to Liz was even stronger than he'd imagined.

"Hello, Mrs. Foster. I'm Ryan Callahan."

"Oh." Her eyes widened in recognition, and she tried to peer around him to see if Liz was there too. "I thought I said to call me—"

"Angela." He let out a relieved breath and smiled. "She's not here. I'm hoping you and your husband can spare me a few minutes of time."

She glanced over her shoulder and opened the door wider. "Come on in." After wiping her hands on her slacks, she led him into the house toward the adjacent living room.

As Ryan stepped into the room, a casually dressed, slender man rose from the recliner with a frown on his face. Liz obviously got her height and build from her father. "What's going on here?"

Angela coughed. "Dan, dear, this is Ryan Callahan. He's Liz's young man."

Hmm. Not her fiancé? Was that intentional on Angela's behalf, or a mere slip?

"He's the hotshot photographer in the book Liz sent us." Angela twisted her fingers together as she glanced between the two men.

The woman was obviously nervous about this unexpected meeting, but at least this confirmed that Liz's dad knew the book had come from his daughter.

A quick glance of his own established that the book in question sat on the coffee table beside a coffee cup. It had to count for something, since the man hadn't destroyed or hidden it.

Deciding to make the next move, Ryan stretched out a hand. "Pleased to meet you, Mr. Foster."

The man shook his hand with a businesslike up-and-down motion but only grunted verbally in response. Unlike his wife in her letters, there was no invitation to call him by his first name.

Fine. This journey toward reconciliation would be taken one single step at a time.

An awkward silence hovered over the room as they waited for him to state his business—which would be difficult enough without everyone standing as well.

Still wearing his winter coat—and without an invitation to remove it—Ryan glanced at the nearby couch and cleared his throat. "May I?"

Mr. Foster grunted again, then resumed his former seat in the recliner while his wife perched on the other end of the couch. A quick glance around revealed a collection of somewhat dated and worn furniture. And aside from a large, nicely framed photograph of a rugged ocean shoreline, the only other decoration in the room was a spindly artificial tree in the corner. The sparse arrangement of homemade ornaments seemed lonely on the thin branches, and the lack of joy in the room matched the expressions on the faces of Liz's parents.

Since his presence didn't seem very welcome, he thought he might as well skip the small talk and get right to the point.

God? Could You help me find the words?

He took a deep breath and forced a smile to his face. "A paper invitation felt too formal. I wanted to meet both of you and extend a personal invitation to the wedding."

"The wedding?" The frown on Mr. Foster's face deepened.

Ryan willed himself not to flinch. A quick glance at Angela's staring at the hands clenched in her lap confirmed his earlier suspicions. As he'd thought, she hadn't shown the invitation to her husband.

Perhaps he should pretend they'd intended an in-person invitation all along. "Your daughter—"

"I don't have a daughter." Despite Mr. Foster's harsh words, they sounded weak and rehearsed. As if his defenses were crumbling.

God? I need Your help to speak the truth with love and grace. To be patient with this man. This child of Yours.

Ryan sucked in a long breath, then leaned forward to rest his elbows on his knees as he speared the other man with a firm gaze.

"Yes, you do. I read your letter to her, so I already know what you think about—"

"Children should obey their parents."

"Yes, but Jesus also taught that His disciples should be willing to leave behind their family to follow Him."

"That's not why she left." The man's scowl left no doubt as to how he felt about Liz's behavior.

Ryan held up a hand. "I'm not saying she's without fault, and I've only heard her side of the story about what happened back then. All I'm saying is that she found her way back to her faith in God and wants nothing more than to fix what's been broken."

"It would take a miracle."

"Perhaps. But God is still in the miracle-working business." He glanced at Liz's wide-eyed mother beside him, then back at Liz's frowning father. "In the meantime, I've been blessed to get to know Liz. She's an amazing woman with an innate talent behind the camera that she must have inherited from you."

Mr. Foster's lips pinched, and Ryan hurried on. "But, mostly, it's her precious love for God and all His children that makes her so beautiful. She challenges my faith and makes me want to be a better man."

Beside him Angela sighed, but Ryan kept his focus on Liz's father. Was that a softening around his eyes?

"Anyhow, even though I don't deserve her love, Liz has agreed to be my wife. We'll be getting married in Colorado two days after Christmas, and we'd love nothing more than to have you both there to celebrate with us."

Having delivered the bombshell, Ryan glanced between Mr. Foster's now-wide eyes and his wife's downcast gaze. One looked shocked by the revelation, and the other unbelievably hopeful.

"Of course, we'll make sure you get a paper invitation, too, for your scrapbook or photo album."

At this, Angela raised her head to meet his gaze and nodded. Hopefully now she could reveal the previously sent invitation without repercussions from her husband.

The husband who only seemed capable of grunting. And frowning.

Since he was already here, he might as well go all in.

"We'd love to have you come for Christmas as well as for the wedding. In fact, as my gift to Liz, I'd like to pay for your hotel and transportation."

At that, Ryan found himself in the uncomfortable position of making small talk to fill their stunned silence. "At some point over the holiday weekend, we'll have dinner and open presents with my sister, her husband, and their two kids. But you're more than welcome to join us for that happy chaos. Or maybe you already have plans with other family?"

Angela shook her head. "There's no other family." The catch in her voice revealed an element of pain...and reinforced his belief that she was trying not to hope.

Mr. Foster simply frowned and changed the subject. "You're the one who took most of the pictures in the book, right?"

If he needed time to come to terms with the news, Ryan could be patient. "We were about even."

Mr. Foster raised an eyebrow, reminding him of Liz.

Ryan reached for the book. "I can point out exactly which ones were mine and which were your daughter's handiwork. The cover image was a shot I took the last morning we were in Fiji."

The other man nodded, as if only a man's work was worthy of gracing the cover of a professional book.

Ryan gritted his teeth and flipped it open. "I tend to specialize in landscape photography, so the chapter on the island's geographical features is mostly mine." He turned instead to the chapter on family life. "However, Liz has a gift for catching candid expressions, so most of the pictures with people in them are hers."

He pointed to the series of images featuring a multigenerational family working and eating together, both inside and outside their thatched hut in the middle of the jungle. "The matriarch of this family took a liking to Liz when we saw her at the village market. She invited us to spend the day with them out in the jungle, but only if she could teach Liz the skills a proper wife should have—including how to catch, butcher, and prepare the chicken for the evening meal."

Ryan chuckled at the memory, then pointed to the picture of a chicken being plucked. "I actually took this one while Liz was behind the hut, losing her lunch, after the actual butchering." He shook his head. "But she immediately picked up her camera and got back to work—even ate the meal they prepared." He smiled at the memory and examined the other photos. "I especially love this shot of the mother surrounded by her family."

Despite being surrounded by poverty and sandwiched between caring for the elder generation and her dozen children, the weary woman's gaze had been on her husband. And his on her.

Liz had captured the priceless moment that had been made into a two-page spread on its own: a profound moment showing how the love of a family is the same around the world.

He glanced at her father. His expression had shifted a bit, as if he had become lost in thought while staring at the large image. Perhaps he was finally softening toward his daughter and her talent.

Ryan gently closed the book. "I'm blessed to be able to work beside such a talented photographer as your daughter. And I can't wait to see where God takes us in the future." He checked his watch. Not wanting to wear out his welcome, he slid the book back onto the coffee table and stood.

"Like I said earlier, it may be too late to get your blessing on our relationship, but I wanted to officially meet you both before the wedding. You're still more than welcome to come for the ceremony and the holidays."

Liz's dad stayed seated, but he did offer his hand. "I don't think so, but thanks for stopping by." After a quick handshake, he reached for the book about Fiji.

Was that a good sign or not?

Ryan turned toward the exit and found Angela waiting to walk him to the door. Once out of sight of the living room, he glanced down and saw the longing in her eyes. How lonely she must be without family or her daughter.

He gave into a sudden impulse and pulled her into a hug, then whispered in her ear, "Liz doesn't know I came, but I had to try. I know it would mean a lot to her if you could come to the wedding. And to Christmas."

He released her and reached into his coat pocket for a business card, slipping it into her hand. "It was nice to finally meet you in person."

She swallowed hard, then nodded.

Too soon, he heard the door *click* behind him, and the chill outdoors began to seep into his bones. Turning up the collar of his coat, he hurried toward the rental car.

As Ryan drove away, he wrestled with the unfamiliar feeling of rejection. Mr. Foster might have thanked him for stopping by, but he certainly hadn't welcomed Ryan into the family.

The bitter taste of failure soured his mood.

After all his prayers over the past week, he'd be returning home empty-handed. And Liz would spend another Christmas without her family. Without her father's love.

God, please be Liz's Father and lavish her with Your love.

Despite Ryan's valiant attempts, he was incapable of meeting all of Liz's needs. And what kind of a future husband did that make him?

But, no, his job was simply to love her to the best of his ability, and the rest was up to God.

With a flicker of hope in his heart, he couldn't wait to fly back to Colorado in the morning. Back to Liz.

Except he already felt guilty for dodging her questions about this trip and had hoped to return with better news as a happy surprise.

What would he say to her now?

CHAPTER FOUR

At exactly ten o'clock on Wednesday morning, there came a quick *tap-tap* on the door of Liz's apartment.

If God answered her prayers, she'd have an explanation. But if Ryan continued to dodge her questions, she'd be second-guessing their impending wedding while devouring a carton of Triple-Ripple Fudge ice cream.

After a deep breath, she opened the door, letting in both her fiancé and a blast of wintry air. A shiver made its way up her spine at the frown on his face.

"What's up with the mysterious text message?" Ryan shrugged out of his coat and leaned down for their usual kiss, but she turned at the last moment so that his lips only grazed her cheekbone.

She stepped away on the pretext of leading the way to their bargain couch. "I didn't want to have this conversation over the phone."

"Uh-oh. That doesn't sound good." Ryan sat at one end of the couch facing her.

Liz hugged one of the decorative pillows over her churning stomach and fought to keep her voice from cracking. "It's just under three weeks until the wedding. My bridesmaids are throwing a bridal shower tonight. And you're hiding something big."

"I'm what?" His protest might have been believable if his eyes hadn't avoided hers, darting instead toward the fireplace.

"Hiding something." She waved a hand to recapture his attention. "And it all started with this sudden trip you took on Monday. The one you can't seem to find time to tell me about."

His eyes widened and his Adam's apple bobbed. "Maybe I'm trying to figure out why you'd leave six voice-mail messages and send at least two dozen texts when you already knew I was busy juggling two photography jobs here in addition to the travel. What's gotten into you?"

"A deflection isn't going to work." She tried to pierce him with a glare, but there was no denying the fact that she'd gone overboard in trying to reach him. "At first, I blamed myself for being so wrapped up in all the wedding and holiday details that I didn't have the decency to even ask where you were going. But after two days of nonanswers, it feels like you deliberately don't want me to know where you were."

His jaw tensed, almost as if she'd gotten uncomfortably close to the truth.

Her voice rose. "I want to be able to trust you to go on a trip without me being there, but I have to admit, my imagination was going more than a little crazy while you were gone to some mysterious place. And all because I had no idea who you were with or what you were doing. Was it work or a pleasure trip? Were you picking up a present for me? Getting something for the apartment? Or was it a last bachelor hurrah with the guys from the main office?"

Wow. Her insecurities had emerged again in all their demanding, needy, high-maintenance glory.

She bit her lip to stop talking and squeezed the pillow in her lap tighter.

"You certainly have an active imagination." A twinkle made its way into his eyes. "But what if I said I had been looking for the perfect Christmas present for my bride?" He stretched out one arm along the back of the couch, almost close enough to touch her shoulder.

An uncomfortable silence hovered between them as she bit her lip. Could he be telling the truth? After all, it was the season for buying and wrapping gifts. And sometimes keeping those types of surprises required creative dodging.

Yet she wasn't ready to let go of her suspicions—or her anger—so easily. "Then I'd have to say it's a good thing I don't have access to your personal bank account log-ins, because I was more than tempted to see where you'd spent your money this week."

His eyebrows rose. "You were going to log in to my account to spy on me? What kind of trust is that?"

She sucked in a quick breath. *Oh no.* What if he started to have second thoughts about her? "Why am I such a mess? I never thought I'd turn into one of those bridezillas on television."

"Well, all I can say is, drop the act, because it's not very flattering." He leaned over far enough to squeeze her shoulder. "Mind telling me what's really going on? This isn't just because I took a last-minute trip without giving you the itinerary first."

"I hate being lied to. You know my history. Jerry the Jerk lied to my face and behind my back…and it destroyed the relationship I had with my parents." She abandoned the pillow and reached out to clasp his hand between hers. "I don't want there to be any secrets between us because of the damage they can cause. But that's not the only reason I…"

"You…?"

She dug deep for the rest of the truth. "I was also jealous because you got to travel once again while I was stuck here, handling the mundane details. It reminded me of when I watched Cheryl's kids so you could fly to Hawaii."

"But staying here was your choice."

"Just like now, when I said I'd organize the wedding while you handle the business." She puffed out a frustrated breath. "Part of me knows this arrangement is just for a few weeks and I'll be back traveling the world soon, but I can't help but wonder how I'll feel down the road when we have our own kids and I'm left behind with diaper duty."

He shifted her grip until their fingers were intertwined and then used his free hand to lift her chin so their gazes locked. "We're both young, and I'm in no hurry to start a family. Let's just enjoy this season for a few years. Then, down the road if God blesses us, we could always shift our focus to local or United States–based contracts while the kids are young." His crooked grin appeared. "Hey, we could be one of those homeschooling, traveling-around-in-an-RV families."

Liz laughed. "That is *not* my idea of fun."

His smile grew. "Me neither, actually. But my point is, dreams change and we might even be sick of traveling by then. So let's just focus on one season at a time." He tugged his hand free and scooted closer before gathering her into his arms. "But in answer to the whole lying thing you were so worried about, I'm sorry I didn't tell you where I was going. I thought it would be a perfect surprise and you'd be so happy with the outcome that you'd forgive me for being a little sneaky."

"A *little* sneaky?"

"Hey, give me some credit—I told you I was going on a trip. I could have pretended I was still in town but busy." His deep sigh jostled her entire body a moment before his lips brushed across the top of her head. "I wanted to be Superman coming to your rescue, but on the way home, I realized that rescuing is not my job. Sometimes God is the only One who can handle certain things."

"What things?" Her heart pounding, she eased out of his embrace far enough to see his face. "Just tell me."

"I knew you were missing your mom and the whole lack-of-an-RSVP issue bugged you."

She caught her breath. Could he have gone to Kansas?

"I had this crazy idea to make the wedding perfect for you by getting your parents to come. And since letters can only go so far, I thought it might help if they met me in person."

He had faced their rejection. For her. Tears welled in her eyes.

Ryan brushed a few wisps of hair away from her cheeks, then cradled her face in his hands. "But I didn't want to get your hopes up by telling you where I was going. I wanted to surprise you, and instead I somehow made things worse between us."

A wrinkle appeared between his eyes, and she leaned forward to kiss it. "It was a sweet thought, and I'm sorry I ever doubted your motives. Forgive me?"

"Only if you forgive me." His lips covered hers in a kiss, sealing the incident behind them. A few heated moments later, he shifted her back to her end of the couch and moved to put distance between them.

She fought to steady her breathing, then stole a glance at her muscled—red-faced—fiancé.

"Maybe we should fight more often just so we get to make up afterward."

Heat flared in his eyes. "Down, girl."

A smile bloomed on her face. "You started it."

"And ended it." He softened the reminder with a crooked smile.

She reclaimed the pillow to keep her hands occupied as heat scorched her cheeks. "So, you flew to Wichita. Did you actually get to see my folks?"

Ryan relayed every moment of his visit, stopping often to answer questions about how her mother looked and whether they'd decorated their house for Christmas yet. The eyewitness details stung, especially his description of their somewhat-sparse Christmas tree in the corner beside her mother's upright piano.

Exactly where it always sat when she was growing up.

"Are you okay?"

Liz forced a smile. "It hurts to know they didn't jump at the opportunity to come to the wedding, but I'm glad you tried. Now I don't have to wonder anymore and we can focus on the wedding with the friends and family we have here."

"The whole flight home yesterday, I was hoping you'd react like this."

She raised her eyebrows. "So you truly were planning to tell me about the trip?"

"Eventually. Once I'd worked up enough courage." He shrugged. "But I'm glad you forced the issue."

"So you say..."

He grinned. "I do. But seeing their pathetic tree in Kansas made me wonder whether you'd like to get one for the apartment." He gestured to an open space near the fireplace.

"I'd like to get an artificial one so we have less mess to clean up after the New Year. It's more expensive up front than a freshly cut tree, but it would pay for itself over a few years."

He reached out once more to interlace their fingers on the cushion between them. "I do like the smell of fresh pine, but after seeing the expanse of nature around the world, it's hard for me to fathom killing a tree just for a few weeks of decoration."

"We could always get a can of pine room freshener or scented candles to help pretend it's real. However, I think they now sell trees you could replant later in the yard."

He nodded. "Like a row of Christmas memories to admire year after year." He offered a half smile. "We'll have to buy replantable trees after we find the property we want for our dream house."

Liz grinned at the thought of building a true home together. And yet she couldn't imagine the future seasons of their lives without also picturing a miniature cowboy trotting along behind his father.

"But in the meantime, I'll find a decent-sized artificial tree…and maybe we can get together to decorate it on Saturday morning." Ryan raised an eyebrow as if asking her permission.

She nodded. "I've got other shopping to finish this week, so I can pick up decorations to go on it. Any preferences?"

They spent the next few minutes deciding on a simple theme of colored lights, strings of popcorn, and one-of-a-kind ornaments that meant something to them…like her new snowman ornament to commemorate the day they had gone sledding.

"If you have a hot glue gun, I could try to add hooks or strings to your souvenirs." Ryan waved a hand at the small collection on her bookshelf. "They're small enough to make perfect ornaments for the tree."

"And they hold lots of memories of us together." She smiled so widely, it hurt her cheeks. "What a great idea."

"Plus, with Grant wanting us to take on more books, our collection would grow year after year."

"Starting with a second trip to Argentina."

"Actually, there's the honeymoon first." He waggled his eyebrows.

"Which is in…?" It didn't hurt to ask.

"A place that's still a secret." He winked, then frowned. "As long as you don't consider it lying to keep the location a surprise."

She winced at the reminder of her earlier overreaction, then leaned across the gap to give him a quick kiss. "No. It's Christmas—a season filled with presents that we have to wait to open before knowing what's inside."

"Making our honeymoon yet another gift for us to open together." Ryan's gaze heated, and her face flamed in response.

The dear, sweet man had already given her so much. If only she could think of the perfect gift for him this Christmas.

* * *

Only a fool in love would volunteer to hot-glue anything.

Ryan winced yet again as the scorching tip of the mostly plastic gun oozed liquid fire over his fingertips…and the tiny nylon loop he held in place atop the cluster of palm trees from Samoa.

Hopefully this would be his last encounter with the instrument of torture. In future travels, he'd be on the lookout for ready-made ornaments instead of the touristy bits of plastic Liz had collected.

He set the small figurine on the paper towel beside the row of other souvenirs-turned-ornaments and eased his fingers away, leaving behind a set of fingerprints. And taking away clear strands of glue and aching, reddened flesh.

"Almost done, big guy?" Across the room, Liz lounged at one end of the couch with a giant bowl of popcorn in her lap and a string of kernels trailing from her busy hands down to the carpet. Nearby, her phone broadcast a playlist of traditional carols and holiday tunes.

"Am I done getting burned? Yes. Done with the ornaments? Almost." He yanked the cord from the outlet and left the glue gun to cool on a sheet of newspaper.

"Need me to kiss it and make it better?" Liz's voice held more than a trace of laughter.

He shot a glare her direction, then reached for the package of metal ornament hooks.

Then again, who was he to complain about tender skin, when she'd already pricked her fingers multiple times with the needle? At least he had a few days to recover before needing the full use of his hands to edit the images he'd shot at last night's wedding.

As he threaded the small end of each hook through the various loops and bent the wires to hold them in place, his mind wandered back to the challenge of photographing a wedding alone. The long list of requested shots had kept him moving, but even while he'd arranged the various poses, all he could imagine was how Liz would look at their wedding.

After attaching the last hook, he made a basket with his T-shirt and carried the new ornaments over to the coffee table, where he lined them up beside two coiled strands of popcorn. Despite the burns, the results had turned out quite nicely.

Hopefully Liz would agree.

"Those are really cute." Liz slid another kernel along the string. "I'm about done with this strand, and then I can help put the lights on."

Ryan eyed the six-foot tree he'd assembled while Liz popped the popcorn. "I can't wait to see how it looks once we get it decorated."

"This place will look even more like a home." Liz sighed. "Just in time for Christmas."

Christmas Eve was just two weeks away. After their final fittings in a few days, then the countdown to Christmas would truly begin...with their rehearsal and wedding immediately following.

The anticipation had started to keep him up at night.

Seeking a distraction from the direction of his thoughts, Ryan focused on untangling the lights. By the time he tested them, Liz had tied her last knot and joined him beside the prickly plastic branches. With Liz humming along to the holiday background music, they worked together to arrange the lights evenly throughout the branches, then added the popcorn garland and ornaments.

Except...

"Uh-oh. I think we need another strand of popcorn here at the bottom." Liz propped her hands on her hips and frowned at the tree.

Ryan draped an arm across her shoulders and drew her closer to his side. "It would make it more balanced. But what about the top? Do you think we should get a star, or would you rather have an angel?"

"Hmm." Liz leaned her head on his shoulder, and he inhaled the clean scent of her shampoo. "I'm not sure."

"I think it should be something simple or even somewhat rustic to match the rest."

"Oh." She shifted and her eyes met his. "I saw on Pinterest someone who'd actually put a crown of thorns at the top as a reminder of a different tree."

He grinned. "I like it. It's both simple and rustic, plus it—"

"Keeps our focus on the true Reason for the season." Happy tears glistened in her eyes.

"Which makes it another tradition for us to keep." Using their proximity as an excuse, he dropped a quick kiss on her lips. "Now, how about you work on the last string of popcorn while I see if I can find a crown online?"

"We could string it from both ends, you know." Her lower lip pooched out in an adorable pout that simply invited another kiss.

And then another.

A firm hand on his chest gently pushed him away. "Hold your horses, cowboy. You're not going to get out of popcorn-stringing duty so easily."

He sucked in a quick breath and fought for sanity.

By the time he'd located and ordered their unique tree topper with Express delivery, Liz had set them up on opposite ends of the couch with the popcorn bowl in the middle.

Oh well. Burned fingertips also deserved to become needle-pricked. Especially if it put a smile on his fiancée's face.

Ryan watched Liz's method, then concentrated as he pushed a sharp needle through a fluffy kernel. The piece of popcorn broke before he could push it farther along the thread toward Liz. Guess he'd just have to eat the evidence.

"As you see, there's a learning curve." Liz giggled.

He reached over to tickle her sock-clad toes before turning his attention back to the task at hand. Between the music, the newly decorated tree, and the company, he soon found himself relaxing against the cushions as the strand of popcorn steadily grew. "You're right. It feels like a home here."

"I can't wait for you to be around all the time." A delightful blush spread across her freckled cheeks.

It was a good thing his hands were occupied. Still, he poured the depth of his feelings into a slow wink before deliberately turning the conversation toward the time line of moving the rest of his things into the apartment.

When he'd put his career on hold last winter to move in with his sister and help out while her husband was deployed, he'd put most of his things into storage. So once Liz had leased the apartment, he'd emptied his storage unit to help her get a jump-start on furniture.

"What's left in your room at Cheryl's house?"

"I can bring all my clothes over on Monday, the 26th. Well, everything but a couple of pairs of jeans and my suitcase for our honeymoon."

She raised an eyebrow. "When are you going to tell me what I'm supposed to pack?"

"Maybe I'll ask Dani to pack for you." He snuck a glance in her direction.

"What?" Liz threw a handful of popcorn at him. "That's not fair."

"Hey, you told me surprises were okay." Ryan gathered the popcorn and added it to the string before turning the conversation back toward moving. "I've still got a few of my favorite framed photos hanging up at Cheryl's."

"Those can come over any time."

"Sure. Then all that remains is my camera equipment and the business setup. As soon as I finish editing the pictures from last night's wedding, then I can go ahead and set up an office in the spare bedroom."

Liz tied a knot in her end of the string and returned her needle to the sewing kit open on the coffee table. "I think this is long enough, so if you want to tie off your end, I'm going to make some hot chocolate. Want some?"

"If you're making it from scratch, yes; otherwise, I'd rather have a cup of strong black coffee."

Liz laughed as she stood. "No more prepackaged mixes for me. Cheryl showed me the 'secret recipe' on the side of the can of Hershey's Cocoa, and I might have become a bit of an addict."

Ryan strung the last kernels in his hand and happily tied a knot of his own. After draping the strand over the bottom branches of the tree, he decided to clean up their decorating mess and picked up the empty Christmas-tree box. "I suppose this box can go in the spare bedroom for now. Might as well check out the space to see if—"

"Don't go in there." Liz dashed over from the kitchen and blocked his path down the short hall.

"What? Is it a mess, or are you now the one keeping secrets?" He grinned to soften his teasing.

Another blush raced across her face. "No. It's just a surprise."

"Now my imagination is going wild...."

Liz executed the perfect eye roll. "I just don't want you to see the veil and stuff that goes with my dress before the wedding."

Ah, yes. The wedding.

He dropped the box against the wall and backed away from the room-of-secrets. "Then I'll let you put this in there after I'm gone."

However, her words sparked an image of her walking down the aisle toward him while surrounded by friends and family.

But Liz would only have friends there. At least until they said their vows and he became her family.

No. She already had a family, with God as her ultimate Father. But that didn't mean Ryan couldn't also help give Liz all she needed.

No matter his motives—and even though she'd admitted that she'd overreacted—it would take time to fully rebuild her trust after his hasty trip to Wichita had raised doubts about his honesty.

He never wanted to hurt her again, and he'd do whatever it took to keep a smile on her face.

CHAPTER FIVE

The following Wednesday found Ryan placing his collection of specialty camera lenses into their foam-lined boxes.

Never had packing felt so good. In fact, he should be able to move all of his equipment out of Cheryl's house in a single trip.

And then, as Hannah would say, just thirteen more sleeps until he was a married man.

A smile stretched across his face. He might miss spending time with his niece and nephew, but he was more than ready to trade their antics for a lifetime with Liz.

With the lenses safely stowed, he turned his attention to packing his laptop's external hard drive and the box of flash drives. Just as his boss and mentor had taught him, all the pictures he took had been transferred from the camera's memory card onto his laptop and then backed up in several other locations, including to a digital cloud.

A quick glance confirmed that the labeled flash drive from Friday night's wedding was on the top of the stack. Of course, he'd already loaded the edited images onto the password-protected website so the happy couple and their families—including Cheryl's next-door neighbor—could order prints. Hopefully they would place their orders quickly so he could finalize everything before Christmas.

Because the next bride he wanted to see was his own.

That reminded him of the lengths Liz had gone to so he wouldn't see her veil or any of the trimmings before their special day. The way she'd planted herself in front of him and the Christmas-tree box still made him smile.

Last night on the phone, Liz had said the spare bedroom was now available to set up as an office. Just as long as he promised not to peek into her—soon to be *their*—bedroom.

Ryan slid the lid onto a filled rubber-storage tub and carried it out to his truck. Just a couple more tubs to pack and he'd be ready to move his equipment into the apartment and lay claim to at least one of the rooms. Of course, he'd still need to measure the wall space before shopping for office furniture, but organizing the room would keep his mind off a certain redhead and her delicious lips.

Halfway back to Cheryl's door, his phone rang. He pulled it out and glanced at the unfamiliar number. If they were calling about a photo job, they were out of luck because his calendar was now booked solid for months. Still, it was never a good idea to burn a professional bridge.

He stepped inside the warmth of the house and swiped the screen to answer. "Ryan Callahan here."

"Oh, good. It's you." A woman's voice filtered through the speaker. "This is Angela Foster, Liz's—"

"Liz's mom." He stopped in his tracks. She'd actually called the number on the business card he'd given her. "Is everything all right?"

He caught the wisps of a shaky breath over the line. "Is your offer of a place to stay in Colorado still available?"

"Of course."

"Well, Dan finally got around to asking what I'd like for Christmas." Angela's airy laugh brought a smile to his face. "And I told him I'd like to see my daughter get married."

"Really?" *Please, God, let this be what I think it is.*

"He might say it's only for my sake, but honestly I think it relieved his pride to have an excuse to make the trip. But I wanted to make sure it was still all right with you."

"It's more than all right." Ryan strode down the hall into Cheryl's kitchen and reached for the pen and paper his sister kept beside the refrigerator. "Let me know when you're planning to arrive and how long you'll stay, and I'll book a hotel for you. Can I text you the confirmation number or would you prefer e-mail?"

"E-mail is fine." She rattled off an address and he hurried to keep up on paper. "I'd like to come next Friday and leave the morning after the wedding. Or is five too many nights? Because we—"

"No, that would be perfect." Especially since it meant they'd be around for Christmas too. He quickly jotted down the dates. "Now, do you want to fly out or—"

"We'd rather drive. Airports are too much hassle over the holidays, and Dan said we can make the trip in about eight hours."

"Weather permitting."

"So far it doesn't look like any big storms are brewing in the forecast."

"We'll pray it stays that way...." Ryan drew a circle around the dates on his note and grinned. "Liz is going to be so excited to hear—"

Angela gasped. "Please don't tell her."

"What?" His stomach knotted. "I thought you said your husband agreed."

"He did. I'm just afraid he might get cold feet or be stubborn and change his mind. And while missing this trip would just kill me, I don't want Liz to be extra disappointed right before her happy day." Her voice cracked. "There's been enough of a shadow on their relationship without adding an extra wound."

Ryan rubbed his forehead. "So we wait until it's for sure and then surprise her?"

"Please? I know you're already the one paying the bill, but could you just do this one more thing for me?"

With just one request, he found himself in a difficult position between his bride and his future mother-in-law. Which one should he keep happy at the expense of the other?

No wonder there were so many mother-in-law jokes floating around.

He sighed. "I promise I won't say anything to Liz." *For now.*

"Thank you. This is going to be the best Christmas ever."

A smile returned to his face. "It will be good to spend more time with the both of you. I'll get to work on the hotel reservation and let you know the details."

Ryan hung up a moment later and stared at the phone in his hand. Had that really happened? Were her parents truly coming for both Christmas *and* the wedding?

The miracle within reach, he fought his impulse to dance like Hannah around the kitchen. He couldn't wait to see the smile on Liz's face when he finally told her.

And yet, until then? Ugh. He hated to keep this secret from her.

But not telling her about her mother's call wasn't really a lie, was it? Maybe it was just another Christmas gift for under the tree, and Liz had agreed that surprises like presents were fine.

His stomach knotted with guilt over twisting her words.

God, please let the days pass quickly.

Maybe it would be better to simply avoid spending time with Liz. He could always blame his absence on unbearable temptation whenever they were together. Especially since it was true.

But when he had to be around her, he'd just keep the topics of conversation to his moving and their Christmas celebration plans. If all else failed and she got suspicious, he could always reveal their honeymoon destination.

He gritted his teeth. He'd do whatever it took to keep the topic off the guest list so he wouldn't have to lie in order to honor his promise to Angela. Suddenly, somewhere in the back of his mind was a lingering memory about seating charts for the reception and head counts for the caterer. Would keeping Angela's secret mess up the wedding reception?

If only he could ask Liz for more information without giving away his reasons.

Ryan channeled his frustration into carting another heavy box of equipment outside and stopped just short of tossing it into the bed of the truck.

Wait a minute. He didn't have to ask Liz. Dani would know the answers and could easily offer to help Liz with the final details, therefore keeping the extra guests a secret.

With a new spring in his step, Ryan returned inside for his last box of equipment. He had just shoved it across the open tailgate when another thought stopped him cold.

What if it slipped out somehow that he was secretly talking to Dani? No. It was too risky. Especially since the bridezilla version of Liz had already questioned whether he was trustworthy.

Unless… He slammed the tailgate shut. What if he talked to Dani about a Christmas gift idea too? Then they could honestly say that's what they talked about and avoid any lies.

Not to mention, he might actually need a backup gift just in case the main surprise fell through.

* * *

"How many more days until you say 'I do'?" Dani grinned across the table at the pancake restaurant.

"Does today count or not? I always get confused." Liz frowned as she tapped her fingers on the chipped Formica surface. Today was Saturday. Next Saturday was Christmas Eve, so that made seven more days. And then Christmas and the rehearsal on Monday—

"And here I thought you'd know...."

Liz rolled her eyes. "It's easier to do what Ryan does. He picked his niece's brain and is counting sleeps."

Dani merely raised an eyebrow as she sipped her coffee.

"As in, exactly ten more times I go to bed a single woman..." They shared a smile, but Liz still felt heat rising in her face.

"The hormones are the toughest part of the countdown, but at least you've got Christmas in between to help distract you."

The waitress picked that moment to bring their food. Liz's mouth watered as she drizzled homemade strawberry syrup over her short stack.

Dani giggled. "Are you still going to fit into your dress with all those carbs?"

"Very funny." Liz took a bite and let the sweet flavors swirl in her mouth. "Thanks to all the wedding stress, I've been getting in extra workouts. Not to mention, I had the seamstress leave a little breathing room around the middle so I wouldn't have to deny myself any Christmas cookies."

"As long as you've planned ahead." Dani took a bite of her omelet. Ever the dancer, she took her protein intake seriously. "So what's your handsome cowboy doing this morning?"

"Playing carpenter." Liz pictured the tool belt hanging low around the waist of his Wranglers.

"It's a step up from the glue gun." Dani winked.

After Tuesday's dress fitting, her best friend had helped transport her wedding gown back to the apartment...and then oohed and aahed over the decorated tree. Especially the custom ornaments Ryan had made.

"True. Today he's armed with a real hammer and several screwdrivers. We went shopping yesterday for desks and bookshelves for the office, but he's insisting on putting them all together by himself. In fact, he almost pushed me out the door to meet you for breakfast."

"What? You could have handed out tools and read him the directions."

"And diminish his man card?" Liz laughed at the thought of her cowboy studying printed diagrams when he would rather figure it out instead. "I also could have mopped his brow and made cookies to go with his coffee when he needed a break from all the manliness."

"And if he happened to hit his thumb with a hammer, you'd have been there to kiss it and make it better." Dani's chuckle faded. "However, he might be worried about the alone-together-in-the-apartment-with-only-ten-sleeps-to-go temptation."

Liz felt her face burn. Lately their kisses had grown more intense, and it had been harder and harder to let go. "There was a special look in his eyes when he kissed me goodbye at the door...."

"But...? You hesitated."

"The physical chemistry certainly sparks when we're together. But our conversations lately are almost superficial, and I can't shake this feeling that he's avoiding me."

"By coming over to your apartment?"

"Or maybe he's hiding something." Liz swirled another bite of pancake through the puddled syrup as she mentally replayed their conversation after his unsuccessful trip to Wichita. The day she'd overreacted about his lack of communication. The day they'd agreed the only acceptable secrets were gifts and happy surprises.

She sighed. "Maybe I'm being paranoid and it's just about a gift."

An odd expression crossed Dani's face.

"You know something."

"Who? Me?" Dani dug into her fruit cup as she avoided eye contact.

"Yes. You. Know. Something." Liz punctuated each word with a pointed finger.

Dani batted away the accusing hand and smiled. "Well, if you must know, he might have called me to ask about Christmas-gift ideas for you...."

"Oh." What was she going to do about her highly suspicious mind? She really should—and could—trust Ryan's love for her. "I'm an idiot. Forget about my crazy ravings, or blame them on my being a stressed-out bride."

"I know the feeling, and you're forgiven." Dani's smile underscored the truth of her words.

"So, a Christmas-gift idea?"

"Beg all you want, but my lips are sealed."

"Did he mention anything *he* might like?" Liz polished off the final bite of her breakfast and pushed the empty plate aside.

"What? Miss Organized doesn't have her shopping done?"

Liz grinned, then rolled her eyes. "Actually, his gift is hiding in my closet right now…behind the garment bag with my dress. And he's under strict orders not to go into the bedroom, because he knows I don't want him to see the dress until the wedding."

"Right. So what did you get Ryan?" Dani popped the last blueberry into her mouth.

"Why? So you can tell him?"

"No, I might still need an idea for Alex."

Liz motioned for the passing waitress to refill her coffee. "I doubt Alex needs industrial-strength luggage in a bright yellow color that won't get lost in Baggage Claim." There had been a few long waits in airports while sifting through mountains of bags, trying to locate theirs.

"True. Any other ideas?"

"Well, if you were half as addicted to caffeine as we are, I'd suggest an 'international coffee of the month' club. I almost went that route for Ryan, but I didn't want packages getting lost while we're—" She caught a fleeting look in Dani's eyes. "Does my gift have something to do with coffee?"

Dani executed a perfect eye roll of her own. "Do you seriously think I'd tell you, even if it did? I was just thinking about you traveling so much and the fact that you'll probably beg me to pick up your mail while you're gone."

"If you don't mind."

Dani shook her head. "That's what friends are for. Just make sure I know the dates."

"We can handle the short trip for our honeymoon, but then Argentina is next." With even more countries on the horizon to fill up their spring. However, this time, when the main office made the travel arrangements, they'd only be booking one hotel room instead of two. The next few months would feel like one long honeymoon.

"I saw your smile."

"Just thinking about our honeymoon." Liz took a sip of her fresh coffee. "When you talked to Ryan, did he say anything about where we're going then? He threatened to have you do my packing."

"He did ask if I'd be willing to help you pack." Dani's grin widened. "But he was right about one thing: you'd be a nagging mess of questions if you thought I knew anything more...so he wouldn't tell me a thing. Said I didn't need a week to pack a simple suitcase and he could tell me later."

A frustrated groan escaped Liz's lips. "This waiting is killing me. Whose crazy idea was it to get married after Christmas anyway?"

"Yours. I seem to recall you being too busy hopping from country to country to do the planning you thought was required."

"True." They could have already been married if she hadn't insisted on waiting until she could organize a picture-perfect wedding. And in the meantime, both she and Ryan struggled to keep their relationship pure.

Just ten more sleeps.

Liz took a deep breath and shifted the conversation toward Dani's Christmas plans. "Have you and Alex finally decided on how to decorate your apartment for the season?"

As she listened to Dani chatter about compromises, married life, and how they needed to weave their family plans around the theater's show schedule, Liz still found her mind wandering to what her future with Ryan would be like.

And then the doubts crept in.

Would she be a good wife? Was Ryan truly the right man for her? Had Mom ever worried about making the right choice before marrying Dad?

If only they could be here so she could ask. And so her father could walk her down the aisle.

Obviously, some things weren't meant to be, including her desire for a wedding like the one in her childhood dreams.

Except for the groom. He was everything she could have prayed for.

The same God who had brought Ryan into her life would continue to meet all her needs. Plus He'd promised to give her the desires of her heart. And right now her desire was to be a loving wife and part of a couple that pointed other people to God and His amazing love.

That had to be enough of her fairy tale come true. Right?

CHAPTER SIX

R yan settled deeper into the cushions of his sister's couch and adjusted his grip on the Bible splayed open across his knee. Paired with the festive decor across the room and the steaming mug of coffee beside him, there wasn't a better way to start a new week.

Especially in the quiet of an empty house with the kids at school, John at work, and Cheryl out running errands.

He took another sip of liquid energy, then turned his attention to the underlined passage in Ephesians about husbands loving their wives. He'd had a wonderful childhood example, watching his parents, but the challenge to love Liz as himself leaped off the page.

Before he could figure out how to make the reminder practical, his phone vibrated with a call from the main office. A moment later, the ever-efficient Valerie was on the line.

"Are you calling with more details for the Argentina trip?"

"I have two reservations yet to confirm but will send the detailed itinerary before the end of the week. However, keep in mind that the team from Production probably won't send the final list of requested images until sometime after the first of the year."

"Just in time for us to hop on a plane."

"Call it airport reading material, but promise me you won't peek at it during your honeymoon." His boss's secretary chuckled.

Ryan laughed with her. "Liz might kill me if I let thoughts of work interrupt our trip. Speaking of which, thanks again for pulling a few strings and landing us a five-star hotel on the beach."

"I still wish I could come for the wedding, but with my newest grandbaby due any day now—"

"You need to be there." Ryan took a sip of his cooling coffee. "So if this isn't about Argentina, what can I do for you?"

"I found you another five-star deal to impress your future in-laws."

"You did?" He pushed aside his Bible and leaned forward to rest his elbows on his knees. "I knew it was a long shot this close to Christmas—"

"True. But they just released the VIP inventory." She quickly relayed the details and his new confirmation number, with a promise to immediately follow up via e-mail. A moment later, his phone dinged with a notification.

A quick swipe later, Ryan stared at the invoice numbers. "I've got it, and thank you so much. You're a saint."

"You'll stop by and say hello the next time you're in the area?"

"That's a promise. Liz can't wait to meet everyone in the home office, so I think we might need to squeeze it in after Argentina."

"I'll see what I can do." A tapping sound filtered over the line, as if she were already adding a scheduling reminder to her never-ending list.

After ending the call, Ryan canceled the previous reservation he'd made for the Fosters. Now thanks to Valerie's magic connections, Liz's parents would have twice as nice a room plus a full breakfast buffet. All for the same price.

He quickly texted the change in plans to Angela, then forwarded sections of the confirmation e-mail from his phone. After all, they didn't need to know how much he was spending to surprise Liz.

Could this expense be part of loving her as himself? After all, if his parents were still alive, he'd make sure they were at the wedding.

A quick glance inside his banking app confirmed that he had enough in his checking account to cover all the hotel charges without transferring anything from savings.

He and Liz had made about the same income during the last few trips. And while she'd been paying for the apartment and utilities on her own, he'd been paying for the wedding and honeymoon from his account. Not that either of them could be considered rich, but they'd both been blessed with more than they needed.

However, with their biggest expenses almost behind them, he was more than ready to stop spending money and start earning—and saving—the big paychecks again.

Well, to be honest, he also itched to get back on the road and travel. The stay-at-home banquet, wedding, and basketball pictures had been a trip down memory lane from the season he first met Liz, and his two quick solo trips to shoot locations in the US were a nice change of pace, but he could hardly wait to travel with her again.

To fully be a part of her life.

To be able to look at her without battling the direction of his thoughts and struggling to keep his hands where they belonged.

Just eight more sleeps until she was finally his wife.

And just four sleeps until her parents were officially on their way. He could already picture the smile on her face.

However, just because the Fosters were coming, it didn't mean their family relationship was fully healed. But at least it was a step in the right direction. Starting with a pampering hotel experience thanks to Valerie and the home office.

Dear God, please let their hearts be receptive. He pictured his fiancée's red hair and occasional fiery temper. *And help everyone to guard their words so we can have quality conversations.*

In the middle of his prayers, his phone buzzed with a call from his soon-to-be mother-in-law.

"Hi, Ryan. I got your message, and I wish I had better news." Her voice broke, and a twinge of fear skittered across Ryan's skin. "I don't know whether it's food poisoning or a stomach bug, but it's going on twelve hours and Dan can't keep anything down. I'm not doing so great myself, but I just feel sick at the possibility that we might not be able to come. I even got a new dress, but now…"

Ryan's mind raced with the mental math. If it was a 24-hour virus, they'd have at least 48 hours to rest up and regain their strength before making the eight-hour drive on Friday. "I'll certainly be praying he gets to feeling better soon, but if you need to come a day later or divide the drive into two shorter days—"

"I'll have to let you know." She made a weird gagging noise. "Goodbye."

The call ended abruptly and Ryan collapsed back against the cushions, feeling a bit sick to his stomach himself at the thought of their illness…and the fact that they might not make the trip after all.

He'd been so close to having them at the wedding to surprise Liz, and now everything was up in the air again. Plus, even if they were able to come, what if they were still contagious and Liz got sick right before the wedding? He'd traveled before while battling a stomach issue, and it wasn't anything he wanted to repeat or have her experience.

And he'd been worried the weather forecast at the end of the week might disrupt their travel plans. In fact, he'd been praying the forecasters were wrong about the light flurries heading their way. But now?

God, You've got to take this. I can make reservations and plans, but only You can control the weather. And our health. Please, God, clear skies. Healing. Restore strength and energy and stamina for them to be able to drive. And heal their relationship with Liz in time for Christmas.

Prayer helped ease his stress over the unknown factors. Now he could only wait and see…and keep praying. With new determination to let God handle the Fosters, Ryan turned his attention to his bride-to-be.

At least she didn't have the additional worry of knowing that her parents were sick and might not come to the wedding after all. But he still recalled her talking about the long list of last-minute tasks for this week, including things like wrapping gifts for his family and baking. And something about tying ribbons around the tops of tiny bottles of bubbles.

If he was to love his wife as himself, he might as well get some extra practice now by lending a helping hand to ease her burdens. Even if it meant enduring a debate about what color the reception mints should be.

But with Liz's dad sick and currently unable to travel, first he needed to make a quick detour to buy his backup gift idea after all.

* * *

After her morning workout and a shower, Liz emptied the last of the coffee from the pot into her favorite mug and then curled up on the couch to do her homework before their final premarital counseling appointment the following night.

The pastor wanted them to read—and later discuss—what Paul had to say to husbands and wives. Unfortunately, the assigned section in Ephesians flowed right into her father's favorite verses about children obeying their parents. Except Dad seemed to have forgotten the next challenge for fathers not to exasperate their children.

She sighed and flipped the page to read the beginning of the book and catch the context of Paul's instructions. Before long, she was reminded once again of God's great love.

That He'd chosen her from the beginning.

He'd given her new life.

He'd brought her into His household as His child.

And because of her new beginning, there was also an expectation for her to live a certain way.

A few minutes later, she closed her Bible and hugged it to her chest. Paul had been convinced that living as God's child wouldn't be easy and could even be seen as a battle.

God, keep on reminding me of Your love. When I'm tempted to get mad at Ryan over the little stuff, remind me that we are both Your kids. And You love us both.

Her eyes drifted to the frame hanging near the coat hooks. A birthday gift from Dani, the verse from First John clearly—and beautifully—stated that it was because of God's great love they could be called His children.

Liz had tracked down the artist and bought another verse from Psalm 68 about God being the Father of the fatherless and putting the lonely in families. The smaller frame now hung above her kitchen sink.

God, thank You that I've got a wonderful family full of Your kids. Thank You that Ryan and I are about to build a new family of our own.

Once sweet peace wrapped around her heart, Liz set aside her Bible and reached for her phone with its long list of things she still needed to get done. With a week to go, she'd merged the last items from her wedding checklist into her phone's calendar app so everything was in one convenient place at her fingertips.

If only it weren't still so overwhelming.

She might have stopped by the grocery store last night to stock the pantry with assorted cookie-making ingredients, but she also had a mountain of presents to wrap and boxes of wedding favors to put the finishing touches on. And those were only today's tasks, with more to come throughout the week. *Hmm.* She tapped her finger against her chin. What to do first?

A familiar pattern of knocking at the door derailed her planning, and she hurried to let in Ryan. "This is a surprise. Did I forget something today?" Liz glanced down at her faded sweatshirt, yoga pants, and fuzzy socks.

"No. But I know you could use some help, and I'm just sitting over at Cheryl's with nothing to do." He crossed the threshold into the warmth of the apartment and pushed the door shut behind him. Instead of reaching for her waist after hanging up his coat, he shoved his hands into the back pockets of his jeans.

"What? No kiss?"

"I made myself a promise that if I came over to help, I could only look. But not touch." Ryan's eyes blazed with a heat she'd become more familiar with the closer they got to the wedding.

A heat similar to the one already spreading across her face as she took in the way his clothing hugged his muscular build. She folded her arms behind her back. "Do lips count? Because one quick peck—"

He met her halfway and silenced her commentary with a quick brush across her mouth. Followed by a lingering tug as their lips caught and held a second time.

Who knew kissing without any other contact could be so interesting?

Then their connection was broken as Ryan pulled away and cleared his throat. "If we can't make a rule, then I'd better turn around and leave."

"No, please don't go." She took three steps backward to remove the temptation to wrap her arms around his waist. "I really could use your help, and I've got plenty of other ways to keep our hands occupied."

"Good." He grinned but kept his hands firmly planted behind his back. "What's first on the agenda, boss lady?"

"I like the sound of that." She winked, then waved a hand at the pile of shopping bags beside their tree. "What if we transform my messy mountain into pretty presents first and use the cookie-baking marathon as a reward?"

"As long as I can make a pot of coffee to enjoy with any samples and rejects, then you've got a deal."

"Of course. If you'll get some music going, I'll be right back with the rest of the gift wrap."

Before long, they had developed a system for wrapping and tagging the various gifts for his family and the members of their wedding party. With their hands busy wrestling tissue paper, boxes, paper, tape, and bows, it was easy to fall back into the familiar rhythm of simple chatter and laughter about anything and everything.

But that didn't stop her from glancing his way whenever she could.

And more often than not, she caught him watching her.

Twice they accidentally touched while passing the scissors and once while working together to wrap Matt's bulky skateboard box.

Each contact set off a flurry of tingling nerves across her entire body...and had her holding her breath, hoping Ryan didn't leave. Instead, he simply moved his hands behind his back and gave her a thorough once-over with his eyes.

He certainly took his rule of "look but don't touch" seriously. And yet his blatant visual assessment only fanned the flames of her desire.

Eight more sleeps until touching was not only allowed, but encouraged.

Heat surged to her face at the direction of her thoughts, and she distracted herself with an impromptu wrapping race against Ryan to cover the last two groomsmen gifts.

With time to spare, she added her slim box to the top of the neatly packed tote bag waiting for the rehearsal dinner. Beside it were two cardboard boxes filled with presents for Christmas Eve.

After Ryan selected a bow to adorn the last gift, Liz consolidated the remaining usable supplies to store for the next year. "Thanks for your help. It's a relief to check the wrapping off my list."

"It's the least I could do, since you did most of the shopping for my family." After stowing the last package into the correct pile, Ryan gathered the remnants of wrapping paper and ribbon scraps into a trash bag. "Speaking of family…had you wanted to get a gift for your parents?"

Liz sighed. "I thought a lot about what to get them. And after what you said about their reaction to the Fiji book, I ended up ordering a custom book of our personal photos from this past year." She waved toward the kitchen counter. "It's actually all packaged up and ready to mail even if it won't get there on time."

"But once again, you're doing the right thing and reaching out to them." Ryan crossed the room, then moved her package so it rested atop his coat. "I can drop it off at the post office on my way back to Cheryl's later."

She nodded. "Thanks. So that takes care of all the presents."

"I didn't see one for me." Ryan's face drooped into a pout, but his eyes twinkled.

She almost reached out to slap his arm. "Neither did I. But I'll wrap yours on my own, thank you very much."

After storing the wrapping supplies on a shelf in the office closet, Liz sidestepped Ryan and his trash bag on her way into the kitchen. By the time he had returned from a trip to the outside dumpster, she had her shower-gift cookbook open on the counter beside several large mixing bowls.

"What kind of cookies are we making?" Ryan carefully edged past her in order to wash his hands at the sink.

"I needed something to take to a cookie exchange with my Bible study group on Thursday, but then Cheryl put me in charge of the baking for this weekend as well. She said we needed something for Christmas Eve after the candlelight service and also as a sweet snack between opening presents and the midday meal on Sunday." Liz rolled her eyes. "She probably thought I needed something to keep my mind and hands busy this week. Then again, she might not trust my meal-cooking skills."

"Or she simply doesn't have the patience for cookies. Pies are more her thing." Ryan moved close enough for her to feel his body heat and pointed at one recipe. "I've always liked those pinwheels. They go great with coffee."

"Anything sweet goes great with caffeine." Liz laughed, then studied the directions. "Although sliced cookies would probably be easier to make than cutout shapes and fancy frosting details." She shuddered at the thought of runaway sprinkles in the kitchen. "I don't think I'm in the mood for anything complicated right now."

"Me neither. But I'm just the helper today."

"Pinwheels for sure, then." Liz eyed various recipes as she mentally inventoried her supplies.

Ryan nudged her shoulder and pointed again. "What about those peanut-butter ones with the chocolate kisses on top?"

Her eyes caught his, then drifted to his lips. "Why? Got kisses on your mind?"

He chuckled. "You're not making this any easier, are you?" After another heated glance, he turned his attention back to the pages.

"That's two kinds of cookies. Want to pick one more?"

"Sure. I also like these shortbread snowballs covered in powdered sugar."

"Those are good too." And they also happened to be her dad's favorite. Liz blinked back a few tears.

Would the reminders never end?

CANDEE FICK

CHAPTER SEVEN

On Friday, Ryan spent his noon hour in a hotel lobby, watching the ebb and flow of guests through the glass-enclosed entrance. According to Angela's last text message, Liz's parents should be arriving in the next fifteen minutes or so. Assuming their GPS cooperated.

He was thrilled that they were healthy enough to make the long drive.

And once they were checked in, then he could finally decide whether his invitation had been a good idea.

While seated on a trendy—and somewhat uncomfortable—couch, his right leg began to bounce. More seconds ticked past before he pressed down hard on his thigh. And his nerves.

After almost four years, the upcoming reunion between parents and daughter could go one of several ways. It might be a miraculous fresh start...or simply provide Mr. Foster with the opportunity for an in-person lecture. It would likely fall somewhere—awkwardly—in between.

I know You're probably tired of hearing from me about this, God, but please work a miracle in their hearts and restore Liz's family.

Ryan wiped sweaty palms on the knees of his jeans and clenched his jaw.

The reunion was just the beginning of the weekend. What if they reunited with Liz but didn't like him? He'd only met the Fosters once...

And, God, please let them accept me as her future husband.

At least Liz had been happily oblivious to the fact that her parents were about to arrive. She'd already been under a lot of stress thanks to all the holiday and wedding plans, and he hadn't wanted to add to her burdens. However, now that her list of remaining tasks had shrunk dramatically, hopefully she could appreciate their unexpected company.

Ryan's phone chimed from the pocket of his leather jacket, and he pulled it out in time to spot the scheduled reminder to meet the Fosters at the hotel.

As if he would forget something so important.

He swiped to delete the notification, then opened the app to scan the other tasks on his list. The wedding license was now with the pastor, and he'd delivered the last of the Stewart wedding prints an hour ago. The only critical items left were picking up his tuxedo on Monday, moving his clothes into the apartment, and packing for the honeymoon.

Four more sleeps until they were married.

Maybe today they could both forget about their lists, start to relax, and simply enjoy the moments of the season. Which could mean extra pockets of time to spend with the Fosters…or to comfort his crying fiancée if the visit took on a critical slant similar to the last letter she'd received from her father.

Tired of sitting, Ryan returned the phone to his pocket and rose to pace the perimeter of the tiled lobby floor. Three circles later, the automatic doors slid open and an older couple appeared, wheeling their luggage behind them.

The Fosters had arrived.

God, please let this go well.

Ryan drew in a quick breath for courage and hurried forward. "I'm so glad you made it safely." He exchanged a firm handshake with Liz's dad and tried not to read too much into the man's serious, stoic expression.

Angela, on the other hand, tugged him into a hug—almost as if she needed human contact…or the reassurance that this wasn't a dream.

After a quick squeeze, Ryan released his future mother-in-law and led the way to the registration desk. "Was the weather okay for your drive?"

While the hotel clerk handled the routine check-in paperwork and programmed their room keys, the couple made small talk with

Ryan about road conditions, relatively clear skies, and their overnight stay in Goodland, Kansas, near the state line.

Despite her smile, Ryan couldn't help but notice the dark circles under Angela's eyes. Or her husband's pale complexion. Their recent illness had certainly taken a toll on their health, but they'd still driven quite a distance to get to Fort Collins.

And now it was up to him to be the proper host and see to their needs. "Do you feel up to a bite to eat?"

"I'm not hungry." Angela's voice wavered.

"We stopped just outside Denver for an early lunch." Liz's dad found his first smile. "Although, with the time-zone difference, it didn't feel early."

Ryan grinned. "My stomach doesn't follow time-zone changes either, Mr. Foster."

The man stared for a moment, then grunted. "You might as well call me *Dan*."

Some might call it a minor thing, but he found the breakthrough another in a line of miracles.

"Yes, sir." Ryan smiled, then reached for the handle on their largest suitcase before extending his elbow to Angela. "Since you've already eaten, let's see about getting you settled into your room so you can rest up. We've got too much happening over the next four days for you to overdo now."

Mr. Foster—Dan—raised an eyebrow at Ryan's attention to his wife but quietly followed along on her other side as they made their way to the bank of elevators.

They might not need help carrying their bags, but Ryan couldn't resist the opportunity to see their suite. Especially if it matched the understated elegance of the lobby.

He didn't want to leave without firm plans for the rest of the day, either.

Silence reigned until they'd entered the gold, mirror-lined elevator.

"Now that we're here, what's the agenda?" Dan's voice sounded strained, as if he'd had to force the words out.

Did the man even want to see his daughter?

At Angela's slight squeeze on his forearm, Ryan softened his automatic reaction and looked directly into the eyes of his future father-in-law. "I was thinking of supper together tonight, just the four of us. Then, depending on how it goes, we might stop by my sister's house for dessert. You could meet the rest of the family then."

Dan glanced at his wife, then nodded.

Ryan exhaled his relief yet still found himself rambling to fill in gaps of conversation as the elevator rose toward the sixth floor. "We'll be spending part of Christmas Eve and Christmas Day with them. Of course, after that we've got the rehearsal and wedding with all the additional bridesmaids and such." He forced a laugh. "Knowing how energetic the kids are and how chatty Liz's friends can be, we should probably take advantage of the quiet while we can."

Dan nodded again, but a smile flickered around the edges of his mouth. The elevator doors opened, and he took the lead down the hall.

Once inside their suite, Angela took charge, pointing out where the men should put the suitcases. Then she disappeared through the door of the bedroom with their garment bag.

Leaving Ryan awkwardly alone with his future father-in-law.

Dan glanced around the living-room area with its small kitchenette. "This is quite an extravagant hotel."

And if next week's version in the Bahamas was similar, Liz would love the feeling of home away from home. "I wanted the best for you, sir. Not only is your coming my gift to Liz, but we're about to become family, right?"

Dan raised an eyebrow, as if the thought of Ryan being family was just beginning to sink in. Although, in all fairness, the man had only had a few weeks to come to terms with the fact that his daughter was getting married to a virtual stranger to them.

Ryan kept a smile on his face. "If you're worried about our finances, don't be. We've been blessed with lucrative contracts this past year, plus I got a great deal on this hotel through our company's account. Bricker Communications Group really likes our work. In fact, we already have several contracts lined up over the coming months."

The room fell quiet again as Liz's dad looked lost in thought.

God, please. Please let tonight's dinner go well. Please don't let me offend Dan or give her parents a reason to discredit me.

A minute later, Angela returned and Dan excused himself to use the restroom.

The older woman stepped closer and lowered her voice. "Have you told her yet?"

"By the time you let me know you were truly on the road, she was already on her way to a thing with her women's Bible study group. I did make sure she reserved tonight for dinner with me."

"And now?" Angela's happy smile once again reminded him of Liz's, a delightful fact that eased the knot in his stomach.

"I'm about to make her a very happy woman." They shared a conspiratorial smile. "You've got my phone number in case anything changes, but we'll plan to pick you up around six this evening. Does Italian sound okay, or should we stick with something blander for the menu?"

A gruff voice intruded on their conversation as Dan returned. "Italian actually sounds good."

Angela's smile wobbled. "And I know it's one of Liz's favorites."

"Great." Ryan's glance bounced between the couple. "I'll get out of here so you can get settled and rest up while you have the chance. We'll see you this evening." He headed toward the door.

But he couldn't leave them on such a casual note.

After only a couple of steps, he turned back to face them. "I'm really glad you were able to make the trip after all. And I pray your being here will make this a perfect Christmas for all of us."

Leaving behind a stunned silence, Ryan exited their suite. Bypassing the elevator, he jogged down the hotel stairs and out to his truck.

The time had come to tell Liz that her parents were not in Kansas anymore.

Hopefully she was as open to the idea now as she'd been after his trip to Wichita two and a half weeks ago.

* * *

"Hello, beautiful."

With one hand still on the knob, Liz leaned against the doorjamb and grinned up at her handsome cowboy. "You do have a key, you know. Knocking is not required."

"But it's not officially my home for a few more days. Besides, how else can I guarantee access to the perfect welcoming committee?" He rested his large hands on her waist, backing her into the apartment but also drawing her close enough for a kiss. ·

Their first since Monday's "no touching" rule went into effect.

Liz stole a second kiss while she had the chance. "What's the big idea? You look like you've won the lottery."

"I'm about to." Ryan's lips curved as he eyed her sweatshirt and yoga pants. "However, you're going to want to clean up before dinner tonight. I've got something special planned."

She'd think he was about to propose, except he'd already done that. "What's got you so excited?"

"Actually I've been keeping a big secret."

"A secret?" She fought to keep her smile in place.

"It's a special Christmas surprise for you. And while I wasn't sure it would actually get here, it just arrived, and now I can't wait for you to see it."

She led the way toward the living room. "Shouldn't I wait until Christmas morning?"

"No. They—the present—won't wait long. And you'll want to spend as much time with them—it—as you can before the wedding."

Wait a minute… It almost sounded like he'd gotten her a puppy or another pet of some sort. But, no, Ryan would know better than that since they'd be traveling so much and wouldn't want to ask their friends and family to puppy-sit in addition to collecting the mail.

She glanced over her shoulder and caught the spark in his eyes. He'd apparently been working on this surprise for awhile.

No wonder he'd mastered the art of the conversational dodge over the past week.

But no more.

Liz took a seat at one end of the couch and waited for Ryan to join her. "Did you tell Dani about this gift?"

"Yes." The twinkle in his eyes flashed again and his crooked grin only tempted her to steal another kiss. "I didn't want to get your hopes up in case it didn't arrive on time, but there were certain other arrangements to be made. Dani helped with some of the logistics."

"Are you going to give me a hint?"

"This is actually a Christmas present for your mom too."

"My mom?" She blinked.

"Turns out all she wanted for Christmas was to see you get married."

"My mom? At the wedding?" Tears flooded her eyes and a squeal escaped her lips. "Really?"

The unexpected blessing caught her so off guard, she almost missed the rest of Ryan's explanation about her parents getting over the stomach flu and her dad driving eight hours over two days in order to make it happen.

"Dad came too?" Her initial joy at the thought soured in her stomach. No. She had to hold onto hope for a positive outcome. After all, Dad never went out of his way for anything unless he truly wanted to. "How long have you known?"

Over the next hour, Ryan patiently answered every single question. Twice. And even kept her from pinching herself a third time by breaking his no-touching rule again to hold her hands in his warm grip.

"You have no idea how hard it's been, keeping this a secret. Especially since—"

"Since I freaked out last time." She winced over her previous over-the-top reaction to his trip.

He nodded. "So when your mom asked me to keep it a secret..." He shrugged his broad shoulders. "Who am I supposed to keep happy first? The future mother-in-law or the bride? Whose opinion matters most?"

"The bride's." A line of sitcom-worthy mother-in-law jokes paraded across her mind. "Although I do understand your dilemma, since you want her to like you."

"Forgive me?"

"Of course." She leaned in for a quick kiss but then ducked out of reach when Ryan tried to extend the contact. "Oops. Since we're still holding hands, I forgot about the no-touching rule."

"I forget a lot of things when I'm with you." He took a deep breath, and then a crooked grin flitted across his face. "But if kisses are still out, then I vote to at least keep hand-to-hand contact."

"Deal." Flirting with temptation this close to the wedding wasn't smart for either of them.

But thoughts of the wedding brought back the realization that her parents would be there. Not only was it a huge answer to prayer but also a giant step toward rebuilding their relationship.

Yet the last time she'd actually seen both of them, things hadn't gone so well. What if she couldn't keep her temper in check? What if her dad brought up the past rather than let it go?

She caught her breath, and her heart pounded beneath the college logo on her ratty sweatshirt as other memories returned. Memories of a scathing letter followed by a sob-fest as Ryan held her on a different couch.

"Ryan, I'm scared."

He squeezed her hands. "We're a team now, and I'll be there right beside you. And so will God. He made this all happen, so I've got to believe He's got the details covered."

She sucked in another deep breath for courage. "Can we meet them for dinner tonight?"

"Already arranged."

CHAPTER EIGHT

L iz fingered her gold necklace with the heart-shaped charm as Ryan drove to the hotel. If they were late, it was completely her fault.

Not only had she spent extra time brushing, curling, and then rebrushing her hair until it fell in loose curls around her shoulders, she'd also changed clothes three times before finally settling on her favorite green sweater and a pair of black slacks.

Hopefully she'd nailed the mixture of comfortably casual and classic elegance. Especially since at the last minute she'd added the necklace her parents had given her for her eighteenth birthday.

All in an attempt to capture every boost of confidence possible...and subtly remind her dad that he'd once loved her.

Too soon, Ryan had parked the truck and come around to open her door.

Her stomach churned as he helped her down. "Why am I such a nervous wreck? They're my parents."

"Because you haven't seen them in a long time. But don't worry, I'll be right here beside you, every step of the way." His fingers brushed over the curls she'd loosened from the collar of her coat, then linked with hers before leading the way across the parking lot toward the glassed-in entrance.

Thankfully, their amended no-touching rule now allowed hand-holding, because she truly needed the contact...not only as an anchor for her runaway emotions, but as a distraction from the upcoming family reunion.

"Families get together for Christmas all the time." Then Liz gasped and stopped in her tracks.

"What now?" Ryan's voice held a hint of laughter.

Probably because she was making them even later, though she hadn't meant to stall.

She rolled her eyes. "Because it's Christmas. My parents are here. And my present is halfway to Kansas."

Ryan chuckled and squeezed her hand. "Your package might not have actually made it to the post office."

She felt her eyes widen as she stared up at him. "You forgot to mail it?"

"I didn't forget. I just hoped they'd recover from the flu in time to make the trip after all. So since it might have been late to arrive anyway, I waited." He shrugged his broad shoulders, then tugged her forward toward their destination.

He waited…because he knew presents were better when given in person. And he knew she'd hate to come to Christmas empty-handed.

God, thanks for this amazing man and the way he seems to anticipate my every need.

Her smile grew, and her lips itched to kiss him. However, the doors slid open, so instead of acting on her thought, she followed Ryan into an ornate lobby with vaulted ceilings.

"Wow. This place is fabulous." Her gaze drifted past the scattered seating arrangements and giant planters overflowing with greenery. "But how on earth could my parents afford to stay here?"

Ryan cleared his throat. "It's my gift to them…and to you."

She turned, only to be captured by the depth of emotion in his eyes. "I don't deserve you." A moment later, she spotted an elegant restaurant nestled into a corner of the open space. "But they are going to be incredibly spoiled, staying here."

"I'm glad you like it." Ryan's chuckle held a touch of intimacy as he led them away from the entrance and deeper into the lobby. "It's the same company as the hotel for our honeymoon."

She grinned at the realization that he'd finally given her a clue. But before she could ask what country the other hotel might be in, she spotted her mother getting off the elevator.

"Mom!" Leaving Ryan behind, Liz rushed forward and was soon enveloped in a giant hug.

It was an embrace like coming home, complete with tight arms around her back, a rocking motion, and the hint of moisture against her cheek mirroring the tears in her own eyes.

"I've missed you so much."

Mom squeezed her a bit tighter and drew in a shaky breath. "Me too. It's been too long."

Her grip slackened, and they eased apart enough for Liz to see her mother's face. Even the appearance of new wrinkles couldn't dim the joy radiating from her teary smile.

"Now let me get a good look at you." Mom's eyes skimmed over Liz, lingering a moment on her necklace. "Oh, so lovely. And you look so happy."

Liz felt her smile widen even farther until she thought her face would split under the pressure. "I am happy." From the inside out. And it had all started with the amazing man somewhere beside her.

Thinking to pull Ryan into the conversation, she started to turn away from her mom...and spotted her dad just behind and to the side of Mom.

While she took in the ravages of time and health scares embedded upon his face, another part of her brain registered that his gaze was skimming across her face and hair. Almost as if memorizing her appearance. Drinking in the moments he had missed. Or searching for something to criticize.

No. She refused to go there. She wanted to love him.

And someone needed to make the first move.

Liz sucked in a deep breath and willed her smile to remain steady. As she started to extend a hand, Ryan's nudge against her back had her rethinking her strategy.

She spread her arms wide and stepped forward to greet her earthly father with the same unconditional love God had showed her. At first it was like hugging a tree, all stiff and prickly. Just when she was about to relax her hold, she felt his hands on her back as he tentatively returned the embrace.

"I love you, Dad." Despite the past and thanks to months of prayer, that much was true.

In an instant, his grip tightened and their hug turned into a healing moment. Of course, they still had a lot to talk about, but for now, she was back in her father's arms, and fresh tears flooded her eyes.

Too soon, he released her. Then he reached out to shake Ryan's hand. "Thank you for making this moment possible." Dad's voice cracked with emotion.

Ryan returned the gesture with a smile, then wrapped an arm around Liz's waist. "My pleasure. Now, is anyone else hungry?"

* * *

Two hours later, Ryan hung up their coats in the entryway of his sister's house while Liz finished the introductions.

"It's a pleasure to meet you both. Please make yourselves at home while I dish up our dessert." Cheryl motioned for the Fosters to follow her husband to the living room and then gestured for Ryan to hand over the grocery bag at his feet.

"Just remember that I want some of the Cookies and Cream." Ryan held onto the handles a moment longer than necessary until his sister looked him in the eyes and nodded.

"As if we don't already have enough other cookies to go with the ice cream." Liz laughed. "But, Cheryl, good luck in keeping my mom out of the kitchen."

"She knows me too well." Angela nodded, then followed the other women toward the kitchen. "I wish I'd thought to bring some of my baking...."

While Ryan had been giving an after-dark tour of the town to Liz's dad, he'd been equally aware of her mom's happy chatter in the back seat of his truck's extended cab...and how Liz kept sending heated glances his direction. Attention that left him feeling quite heroic and wishing he could collect her appreciation in the form of kisses instead of glances. And all because he'd had the idea to personally invite her parents to the wedding and through Christmas.

He was loving his future wife as himself.

However, it was God who had planted the original idea, who changed the Fosters' hearts and healed them physically so they could actually come. The same God who had erased the missing years between Liz and her mother.

Thanks to Ryan's eavesdropping on their back-seat conversation, he knew they'd already talked about upgrading their old-fashioned letter-writing to video-chat calls.

Just one relationship left to fully mend.

Belatedly, Ryan followed the other men into the living room, where he found them standing beside Matt, Hannah, and the card table.

"Still working on the puzzle?" Ryan stopped near Dan's elbow and reached out to ruffle Hannah's hair.

"We're almost done, Uncle Ryan." His niece giggled. "And if we finish it tonight, you owe us milkshakes."

"I have to admit, you've made a lot of progress since school let out." He studied the piece in Matt's hand and pointed the boy to an open spot in the left-hand quadrant.

"Can I help?" Dan rubbed his hands together.

"Sure." Hannah scooted off the folding chair and grinned up at them. "Maybe Uncle Ryan will buy you a milkshake too."

"That's okay. Angela put me on a heart-healthy diet, so while I'm getting to cheat a little this Christmas, I think I'd better be safe with just a few cookies for now." Dan actually chuckled as he sat. "You know, when she was a little girl like you, Liz used to sit on my lap while we worked on puzzles together."

Hannah leaned against Dan's leg as she snapped another piece into place. "Yeah. She told me."

Was it too much to hope that, like the puzzle, they could create even more solid connections as they joined their families together?

Three more pieces found their spots before the women returned.

Cheryl set a tray filled with small bowls of ice cream on the coffee table. "The puzzle can wait. Let's have some dessert."

"A puzzle?" Angela jostled a platter of assorted homemade cookies as her gaze flickered to the sight of her husband seated at the card table. A moment later she turned away, but not before Ryan caught a sheen of emotion in her eyes.

He hurried to take two additional folding chairs from Liz so her hands were free to help Cheryl pass out the bowls. With a tilt of his head, he drew her attention to her dad. "Did you see—?"

Her eyes widened, followed by her smile. She quickly crossed the room and laid a hand on his shoulder. "Hey, Dad, I remember when we used to do this."

Dan swiveled and looked up at his daughter. "It's a good memory."

"It is. And I also happen to know that there are a few of your favorite snowball cookies over there."

Interesting. She'd never said so during their baking marathon earlier in the week—but God had taken care of even the smallest detail where Liz and her father were concerned.

Cheryl intruded on the moment as she shooed her children away from the puzzle. "There's time enough for puzzle-solving later. Right now, we've got company." In just a few moments, his bossy older sister had everyone seated and discussing Dan and Angela's drive.

Yet even as his family welcomed the Fosters into their hearts and home, his attention returned to the sight of Liz and her father. They'd come a long way in just a few short hours. First, the memory of their hug in the hotel lobby still gave him chills. And now his Liz continued being open and loving despite her past pain.

Overall, her forgiving nature was a good sign for their future. Especially since he would invariably mess up and make her mad. Wait, he'd already been there, done that, and survived her fiery redheaded temper.

But making up after a fight sure was fun.

He fought the grin spreading across his face as Liz brought him a bowl of his favorite flavor with several chocolate-kiss-laden cookies balanced on top.

Then she sat down close beside him on the couch, and suddenly he was very aware of her dad's gaze on them. Ryan fought the urge to squirm and instead tried to act natural.

As if it was every day he sat mere inches from the woman who starred in all his dreams.

Yet in the middle of his own discomfort, he also sensed that Dan watched Liz especially close, almost as if he was holding back a final decision about her. While their previous dinner conversation hadn't been stilted, it had erred on the side of somewhat-superficial topics.

They were ignoring the proverbial elephant in the room. Then again, just two days before Christmas, who wanted to bring up the issue of having been disowned?

A burst of laughter broke into Ryan's musings and pulled his attention back to his family in time to see a red-faced Matt scooting away from the pile of presents already underneath the tree.

"Patience, son. We'll just need to wait a bit longer." John waggled his eyebrows. "Although maybe your mother will let us open one small gift tomorrow night after church."

"Let who open a gift?" Cheryl rolled her eyes. "Seriously, I don't know which one is the bigger child."

John's smile grew, and after a wink at his wife, he turned his attention to Liz's parents. "You're both more than welcome to join us tomorrow. We're going to the Christmas Eve service at our church at five o'clock, followed by a light meal here with a few classic Christmas movies."

"Like Rudolph and his friend Dennis the elf dentist." Hannah giggled.

"And *It's a Wonderful Life*." Cheryl hugged her daughter before facing Angela. "We'd love to have you along. You could ride with Ryan and Liz, or if you think we'd wear you out, you could drive separately and end the evening early."

Angela's eyes glowed. "The whole evening sounds wonderful to me." She darted a glance at her husband as if asking him to agree.

After a loaded pause, Dan nodded. "We can definitely attend the service with you, but we'll have to wait and see about the rest."

Beside him, Liz breathed out a sigh of relief, and Ryan reached over to squeeze her forearm. God certainly was answering their prayers in baby steps.

"Good." John scooped another bite of ice cream onto his spoon. "Even though Christmas Day falls on a Sunday this year and the church building will be open for a short service, we're planning instead to have a quiet time of family devotions in the morning before we open our presents."

"Once again, you're more than welcome to come for any or all of the chaos, but we definitely expect you to join us for the noon meal." Cheryl pointed her empty spoon toward Ryan and Liz. "Because then we'll shift gears from Christmas to full-on wedding mode and get these two lovebirds hitched."

Hannah wiggled from her spot near her mother's feet. "I get to be in the wedding."

"You do?" Angela's voice wavered, and she turned her attention to her melting bowl of cream.

Right. In the train of conversation over dinner, they'd caught up on the road trip, her parents' vacation, and even her dad's health—especially when he'd avoided the cheese-filled pasta and the second basket of breadsticks. While they now talked about Christmas plans, the wedding details had yet to come up.

"Are you part of my family now?"

Ryan quickly glanced over to find Hannah leaning against Angela's knee and staring at Dan.

Dan frowned a bit, as if trying to figure out the answer. "I suppose when Liz marries your uncle and becomes your aunt, then that makes me—us—something."

"You could be like my grandpa and grandma, since all the others are already in heaven." Hannah nodded as if the subject were settled.

Dan cleared his throat and glanced at his wife. Ryan then followed his gaze toward Liz and found a strange longing in her eyes.

Almost as if she was adjusting to the idea of her parents becoming grandparents. Of course, she and Ryan had previously talked about when they wanted to start their own family, but maybe having her parents back in her life would adjust their time line slightly. If so, he wouldn't mind, as long as Liz was happy.

Sweet Hannah didn't know when to give up. "It's always good to have family around."

"True." Angela's voice cracked as she reached over and took her husband's hand.

"Mommy says Christmas is best when we get to celebrate with the family we have. And this year is even better since Daddy is home." Hannah abandoned her position between the Fosters to give John a hug.

"And I'm very glad to be home." John nestled his nose into his daughter's hair.

Evidently Liz caught a nonverbal exchange between her parents, because she launched into a recap of last Christmas—a season when John was serving overseas and Ryan had come to help Cheryl with the kids. A season that brought him into Liz's life and then brought her back to church at Christmas.

She glanced at Ryan and gripped his hand as she turned back to her parents. "And there I encountered the lavish, overwhelming, sacrificial love of God who sent His Son as a baby. After all, Jesus gave up everything heaven had to offer to come to earth and experience what it means to be human with all our failings and hurts and selfishness and rejections." She took a deep breath. "Because of that unfailing love, I truly found peace for the first time in a very long time. Last Christmas, God changed my life."

As Liz shared her heart, Ryan watched as Angela blinked several times. But Dan only shifted in his chair with a pained expression.

God, please let any seeds planted by Liz's testimony find roots.

CHAPTER NINE

A t the blast of frigid evening air and ice crystals whipping through the church parking lot, Liz tucked her chin into the fuzzy depths of her knitted scarf and huddled closer to Ryan's side. Five careful steps later, they reunited with her parents near the tailgate of their classic sedan.

"Come on." She tilted her head toward the front doors but didn't relax her grip on Ryan's arm. "It'll be warm inside."

"You won't get an argument from me." Her mom shivered beside her as they picked their way across the slippery asphalt.

Behind them, her dad grunted. "All those folks hoping and dreaming of a white Christmas... But when it finally arrives, they complain about the cold."

Ryan chuckled and she felt him turn slightly, as if glancing back at her dad. "True. But at least the snow waited until after today's driving tour. The canyon would have been sketchy if there'd been ice on the road."

Another grunt.

Some things would always be the same, including Dad's pessimistic outlook on life.

By the time they reached the haven of warmth inside the church doors, her eyes and nose were stinging from the cold. Mom's exposed legs had to be freezing beneath the skirt she'd insisted on wearing.

While she'd warned her parents about their church's more casual dress code, she'd forgotten to mention that they served coffee in the lobby. Liz opened her mouth to do just that when she was tackled from behind by a smaller body. She glanced down to find a beaming Hannah. "Merry Christmas, sweetheart."

Her niece-to-be practically bounced with energy, and moments later the rest of Ryan's family joined them. As usual, Cheryl took over and led their combined families toward the sanctuary.

Trailing behind the others as they wound their way through the crowd to find seats, Liz didn't miss the moment when little Hannah squeezed herself between Liz's parents and latched onto their hands—as if they truly were her grandparents.

Dad glanced down with the hint of a smile as the precious girl charmed her way into his heart. On the other hand, Mom didn't even try to hide her grin. Or the longing in her eyes as she soaked up the cheery atmosphere around them.

Liz eyed the friendly people who made up her new church family and couldn't help but recall a particular thread of last night's dinner conversation. Not sure whether she should feel joy, relief, or sympathy, she'd listened to the report about how, after their last congregation sided with Jerry regarding the business issues, her parents had returned to the church of her childhood only to find that most of her mother's friends had drifted away over the years.

God, please be Mom's true friend. The kind that sticks closer than a brother.

Once they'd settled into seats near the middle of the room, Liz took a deep breath and did some atmosphere-absorbing of her own. The happy chatter of families and friends around them blended with the soft instrumental Christmas music playing in the background. All was surrounded by the festive decor of greenery swags, deep red poinsettias, and countless strands of white lights.

Her pulse slowed as her focus shifted once again to the Reason they'd come tonight.

"The wedding will be here?" Mom's voice held more than a few questions.

"Yes." Liz's heart clenched at the reminder that her mother had been absent from the planning. "But we'll add a white runner down the aisle as well as candlestands and a bronze arch with flowers at the front."

Mom's eyes glistened. "It will be beautiful."

Over her shoulder, she caught of glimpse of her dad. He looked around the room, then nodded. Did his nod mean that he approved of the location?

Hopefully her parents would also enjoy the Christmas Eve service. Or at least not get too offended because it was different than the church of her childhood.

She leaned back into her chair, and a moment later Ryan's arm slipped around her shoulders, like he read her mind and knew her fears. Before she could whisper a prayer, the musicians stepped onto the platform and opened the service with a medley of traditional carols.

So far, so good.

But then their denim-clad pastor stepped up to the podium to deliver his message—a message he opened with the words, "Christmas is all about family."

Her eyes flooded with tears, especially when Mom reached over to grasp her hand. And a quick—blurry—glance revealed Mom also holding her husband's hand.

Just like a family.

Their pastor smiled. "I can see—and hear—the families already gathered in this room. But I can't help but acknowledge that some of you are missing loved ones this season. Whether you are separated by death or by choice or by circumstances, this season can be a lonely time."

Her mind jumped back a year to when she'd faced another Christmas without her parents...and been welcomed into Ryan's family circle instead.

"But know this. God sets the lonely into families."

Just like the verse on the wall in her kitchen.

And as though God were trying to underline a theme in her heart, the pastor went on to talk about a section of verses from First John, chapter three, another passage already on the walls of her apartment. "How great is the love the Father has lavished on us, that we should be called children of God... Now we are children of God...."

Two seats down the row, she caught a sniffing sound. Either Dad had a runny nose because of the weather...or perhaps God was working on his heart.

"We now have an eternal family that will never end. This room is full of families...but we're also one big family of believers.

And all because God went out of His way to come after us and bring us back to Him."

Liz snuck another glance at her parents, who both seemed to be paying close attention as the storytelling pastor wove the theme of family into the message. As the pastor shifted the focus of the sermon to Jesus leaving heaven to be born in a stable and found lying in a manger, she felt Ryan's warm hand on her shoulder.

Ryan—a wonderful man who, one year ago, left behind his career to support his family. And who, this year, went out of his way to go after her parents and bring them here. Now. For this moment.

She turned her head to study him and his strong face full of character and conviction. His wide shoulders to carry her burdens. With his obvious evidence of sacrificial love in action for her benefit, it would be the easiest thing in the world to submit herself to his leadership. Just like their pastor had said at their last premarriage counseling appointment.

Ryan must have felt her gaze, because he glanced over with that kissable, crooked grin of his.

Just three more sleeps.

Liz reluctantly turned back toward the front and tried to pay attention to the message. Not long afterward, the service ended with candles lifted high in the darkened sanctuary. And just like last year, she absorbed the sweet embrace of heaven.

Once the lights turned back on, she caught her mom wiping tears from her smiling face. And beyond her, Dad had a few tears in his eyes too.

It seemed God had been doing something in his heart. Their hearts.

As tempted as she was to ask, Liz bit her tongue. Better to let God keep working for now.

However, she still wanted to capture the moment in the way that made the most sense to her. So a few minutes later, she tugged Ryan and her parents over to stand beside a tree in the lobby and asked Cheryl to take a picture of the four of them with her phone. Later tonight she would print the image and put it in a spare frame as an extra gift under the tree for her parents.

And print another copy for over her fireplace.

* * *

The following afternoon, Liz unlocked the door and led her parents into the apartment, with Ryan bringing up the rear and carrying an armload of opened presents.

Mom sighed. "Those kids are adorable, but I'm beat."

Dad actually chuckled as he shrugged out of his coat and handed it to Liz.

"Would anyone like some coffee?" Ryan jostled her new Keurig wedged under his arm.

Liz hung up their coats. "We should probably put that in the office for quick refills when we're working, but right now I think I need more than a single cup of caffeinated magic."

"You don't have to convince me. I'll start a real pot brewing while you show your folks around." Ryan set his load on the counter, then turned to her with a mischievous grin. "I'd give the tour myself, but I'm not allowed—"

"In the bedroom." Her face heated as she faced her parents. "My wedding dress is hanging up in there, and he promised not to peek."

Mom's eyes lit up, and Dad laughed. "Seems she's not as beat as she said."

With only two bedrooms, the tour wouldn't take long. However, they'd hardly gotten past the living room before she described their future plans to save up for property while using the apartment as a temporary home base, since they'd be traveling a lot.

Predictably so, Dad was fascinated by the office setup of Ryan's custom camera equipment and the wood-framed pictures on the walls. On the other hand, once they reached her bedroom and Mom spotted the dress, she suddenly wanted to see *all* the wedding things.

While Dad's eyes glazed over from the girl talk.

She sent him back to the kitchen and then paused to wrap her mother in another of the long line of overdue hugs. "We've got all day tomorrow and Tuesday to talk about the wedding, but I think I need to unwind a bit from Christmas first." Liz fought a yawn. A giant mug of caffeine sounded better and better with every passing minute

"Of course." Mom squeezed her arm as they walked back down the hall. "I'm so happy for you. You've got a beautiful home, and Ryan is such a nice young man."

"God has truly blessed me." Liz's smile grew and she hurried to rejoin the man of her dreams in the kitchen, where he was occupied with getting mugs from the cupboard.

Only after they were all seated around the table and she had her hands wrapped around a dose of the steaming brew did she remember her manners. "I should probably be a proper hostess and set out a plate of cookies or something."

The other three groaned, complained about being stuffed from the meal they'd just eaten, and then resumed their chitchat recapping the morning spent with Ryan's family. Of course, the two main topics were the children...and thanking her again for their presents.

The biggest gift of the season sat across the table from her.

Her family was back together, and there was a new light shining in her father's eyes.

Liz cleared her throat. "You seem different than yesterday." Or the day before. Or, honestly, even in years.

Dad swallowed the last drops of his coffee, then reached out and took hold of her mom's hand. "I *am* different."

Surely that wasn't the only explanation she was going to get.

Liz swirled her half-empty ceramic mug between her hands and risked a glance at Ryan. Should she—?

Dad cleared his throat. "In all the time your mother and I have been married, I've only shared a little of my past with her—things like what state I'd lived in or my high school mascot."

Liz scraped the edges of her memories but only came up with a handful of similar trivial facts. As if any of that explained why he was different today. After a quick glance at her misty-eyed mother, her gaze jumped back to the man across from her.

Dad stared at the woodgrain of the tabletop. "I never told her anything about the hard parts until last night when we stayed up way too late. Of course we spent some time talking about what your pastor had to say about God's family and Christmas, but we spoke mostly about why this time of year has always been a hard season for me."

He took a deep breath, and Liz braced herself for the truth. If he was willing to share it with them.

Her father slowly raised glistening eyes to hers. "I tried over the years to build a family, but just when I thought I'd finally gotten everything in place...you left. At Christmas."

Liz sucked in a quick breath at the four-year-old memories. "You threw me out. At Christmas."

Ryan scooted closer and began to rub a slow pattern on her back, offering his silent support as they finally addressed the main stumbling block in the relationship between Liz and her dad.

She stared into the tear-filled eyes of her father and her heart softened. Pushing aside her cooling coffee, Liz reached across the table and squeezed her parents' clasped hands. "Please. Help me understand."

And, God, help him find the words. Heal his past and restore his future.

With halting words, her dad painted a picture of growing up with a critical, workaholic father who demanded perfection from his family. As a child, he had struggled to measure up, scrambling to stay one step ahead of his father's temper. After his mother got sick, he was accused of wearing her out. Then after she died in mid-December, his father disappeared, leaving a grief-stricken ten-year-old to spend Christmas in foster care.

Her dad's voice cracked. "I bounced around from host to host but never found a place to call home. And I quickly grew to hate my last name, since it had become the story of my miserable life."

Liz winced at the thought of a young Dan Foster also being known as the foster kid. Meanwhile, her mom sniffled a bit, as if she too mourned for the wounded boy she'd married.

"After the third home tossed me back into the system, I blamed myself for breaking some yet-unknown rule from the Bible that particular couple loved to quote. After all, I must have done something to make God mad. Why else would He take away my family?"

"Oh, but God isn't like that." Not the God she'd come to know in the pages of *her* Bible.

Her dad shrugged. "Perhaps. But that's why I was obsessed with controlling every aspect of my life. I became a rule-keeper...desperate to become someone righteous enough so God would stop taking away the people I cared about." He glanced at his wife and squeezed her hand again—evidence of healing in their relationship too.

"I'm truly sorry for all the wasted years I spent trying to be good enough for God to love me. But last night, I finally realized that He already does. Not to mention, God's family is huge and full of adopted kids, like I'd always wanted to be."

Liz blinked back happy tears at the transformation she saw unfolding before her eyes. "God loves us—welcomes us—just as we are. We don't have anything to prove, and nothing we can do will make Him love us more."

Her dad nodded. "I'd been so focused on all I'd lost as a child and then trying to earn God's favor as an adult, well, I was totally blind to the people right in front of me." A smile flitted across his face. "I'd actually had a family for years within the doors of our church. And also with your mother's parents, who welcomed me as their own."

Liz's mind flooded with memories of her loving grandparents and the way her dad had acted around them. Smiling. Laughing. Relaxed.

"So when they both died…"

"It felt like God was judging me again. And then I had to be extra-vigilant so God wouldn't take away their business too. Which is why I was so hard on you…my very own daughter." He blinked back tears, then cleared the emotion from his throat.

"You and your mother were my family. *Are* my family. You're everything I'd dreamed of, and it took a little girl to crumble the walls around my heart."

"You mean Hannah wanting you to be like a grandfather?"

A true smile blossomed among the usual frown-line wrinkles on his face. "She basically told me I should celebrate with the family I *have* instead of dwelling on the ones who are missing."

"And your family is mom and…" Was this truly her official welcome back to his heart?

"And you. If you'll forgive me."

"Of course. I forgave you long ago." Liz pushed back her chair and rounded the table to fully embrace her father, this time without the past looming between them.

Soon both her mother and Ryan joined them for a larger group hug, and the last cracks of her broken heart filled completely.

Ryan chuckled. "If I may be so bold, I'm also about to become part of your family. And if my niece has anything to say about it, you're stuck with my sister's crew too."

Liz's dad eased away from the circle but kept an arm around her mom. "Thanks to my health, we'd already been talking about slowing down or even closing the business. But after last night's service"—he glanced at his wife with a special smile—"we're thinking it might be time for a fresh beginning in a new part of the country. To be close to *all* our family."

Liz's heart double-timed. "Colorado is nice."

"It certainly is." Mom's smile beamed. "Especially because you are here."

Whether they actually moved close enough to spend time with their own grandchildren—eventually—they were both here now, in time for her wedding.

And suddenly Liz knew the perfect place for her father.

"Dad? Would you walk me down the aisle on Tuesday?"

His voice cracked. "I'd be honored."

Tears blurred her eyes as they hugged again. She couldn't be happier.

But then she felt the warmth of Ryan's arm around her waist.

Actually, maybe she could. In just two days.

CANDEE FICK

CHAPTER TEN

On Tuesday morning, Ryan slid into a booth across from his soon-to-be father-in-law. Since Liz insisted he couldn't see her before the ceremony—even accidentally—the men had agreed to meet at a restaurant almost a mile from the hotel.

Today was the day.

He pressed a hand against his churning stomach. The last time he'd felt this mixture of nervous excitement had been the day he'd flown to Idaho to meet a famous professional photographer. That day had changed the course of his life, and this day would do the same.

"You look a bit sick." Dan frowned. "Hope you didn't catch what we—"

"Nope. The waiting is driving me wild." Other than confirming the arrival of his coworker Elijah, he didn't have anything to do until meeting his groomsmen at the church at four o'clock.

"You look almost as wound up as Liz did this morning when she and the girls took over our hotel suite and kicked me out." Her dad's chuckle broke the tension. "Then again, between their plans to decorate for the reception and heading to some fancy salon to get prettified—"

"Prettified?" Ryan felt his lips rise in a half smile.

Dan waved a hand around his head. "You know. The hair and makeup and other froufrou things women think they need for events. But at least all the girly stuff will keep Liz busy and her mind distracted. Unlike you."

The truth hit too close, but... "Maybe it's why I agreed to meet you here. At least we can waste an hour or more over breakfast and coffee." However, when Ryan scanned the menu, nothing sounded appealing. "Actually, I don't think I can eat a thing." He pushed aside the laminated sheet and massaged the knot in his midsection.

"Nonsense. We can't have you fainting in the middle of the ceremony." Dan grunted. "I'll order you something and force-feed you if I have to."

Another smile flitted across Ryan's face at the thoughts of Liz's father attempting it...and Liz's laughter if she ever found out.

Ryan reached for the menu again and finally ordered a three-egg omelet with lots of cheese, hash browns, and a side of bacon. While Dan asked the waitress about heart-healthy menu options and joked about needing to be good now so he could have wedding cake later, Ryan glanced at his phone.

Still no response from Elijah. The man was probably sleeping in after getting into town late last night; they'd laugh later about him needing his beauty sleep. Maybe some of the looming hours could be occupied by going over the list of requested photography shots with the man once he finally woke up.

As the waitress walked away, Dan cleared his throat. "Thanks for meeting me this morning. And not just for an excuse to get away from the giggle-fest."

"I can see how their high-pitched voices would wear on a man's last nerve." He'd spent enough time with Dani and Liz together to know that once they reunited with their former housemates from the theater, well, giggle-fest would certainly describe the resulting noise.

"Speaking of being a man..." Dan studied the mug of coffee nestled between his hands, then slowly raised his gaze to Ryan's. "It took a lot of guts for you to come out to Wichita, not knowing how you would be received. But you fought for my daughter. Not just to get us here for Christmas and the wedding, but you've put her heart first in many other ways. I can see that."

Ryan nodded. He'd tried to be like Christ in his relationship with Liz, and to have his efforts recognized clogged his throat.

Dan's voice cracked. "You supported her dream when I couldn't. When I didn't."

And Ryan had been there to pick up the pieces. Before he could decide how to acknowledge the truth yet still offer encouragement, the other man continued.

"I see now where I've failed as a father, but while I know you'll be the main man in her life from today forward, I still promise to be a better father in the future."

The responsibility settled onto Ryan's shoulders, but he knew only one way to carry the burden. "God is the best example to follow. Get to know Him…and His love in your life makes loving others easier."

A smile flitted across Dan's face. "I know this comes at the last minute, but I wanted to make sure you knew you have my blessing to marry my daughter."

Ryan hadn't known how important his approval was until it was offered. "Thank you, sir."

Dan's brow furrowed. "Liz told me about losing your parents. Maybe someday you'll see fit to call me *Dad*?"

Before he'd seen the man's change of heart, he wouldn't have even considered it. But now? All he could do was nod.

The moment was interrupted by the waitress delivering their food. As he caught the aroma of fried bacon on his plate, Ryan's stomach rumbled. Perhaps he could eat after all.

Two bites into his omelet, his phone rang and Elijah's strained voice carried over the line.

"I'm sorry, man, but I missed my flight. Carol got rear-ended on the interstate and they had to life-flight her to Boston. She didn't come out of surgery until early in the morning and then it was touch and go for a while before she finally stabilized. She was all I could think about."

"As she should be." Ryan shot a prayer heavenward for Elijah's wife and asked for a full recovery from her injuries.

"Even if I felt comfortable leaving her, I don't think I could catch a new flight now and still get there on time."

"Don't worry about it. You need to be with her." Even if it left him without a wedding photographer.

Ryan's thoughts scrambled as he disconnected the call.

"An absent groomsman?"

He shook his head. "No. A colleague who was supposed to be our photographer." But Elijah wasn't the only one from Bricker Communications Group coming to the wedding.

Ryan's fingers flew across the screen as he sent a text message to Grant McHenry, explaining the situation and asking where he was.

A minute later, his boss called back. "A storm over the Great Lakes canceled several flights and delayed others. I'm in New York, caught in the ripple effect. Valerie is working to charter a plane instead, but there's no guarantee I'll arrive in time to be much help."

"I appreciate the effort. Please keep me posted." Once again, Ryan disconnected a call with little hope to hold onto.

"How can I help, son?"

His heart warmed at the label of *son*. He wasn't on his own.

Ryan used his fork to poke at his rapidly cooling food. "I only had two jobs for the wedding: the honeymoon arrangements and the photographer. Failure is not an option, and I need a plan in case Grant can't get here in time."

"Especially when Liz has worked with some of the best."

God, I could use a few ideas here. Who else do I know who can—

Wait a minute.

"You're a photographer." Ryan mentally ran down the list of expected photos. Liz's dad would only need to be in a few of them. And those were shots Cheryl or even John could take. "If I found a different person to take the shots while you walk Liz down the aisle, would you be able to handle the rest?"

"I've really only done school pictures in front of a portable background." Dan stared at his half-empty plate as if ashamed of his level of experience.

Ryan frowned. "But Liz said you have a studio. Surely you've done more than—"

"*Had* a studio. My father-in-law—Angela's dad—opened it long before I came along. But after Jerry stole most of our customer base, I liquidated the remaining equipment. The building is up for sale." Dan blew out a breath as if relieved to be rid of a burden.

Did Liz know that the studio was gone? The future of the business was another topic they'd skirted around before the subject of the wedding took over all their conversations.

"But to answer your real question, simple student IDs or sports-team pictures were all I could manage. I was jealous of my father-in-law's talent. Jealous of my own daughter's. And while I appreciated Jerry branching out and doing creative things to grow the overall business, I stayed with the rut of what I knew how to do." Dan shook his head. "No wonder Liz didn't want to get stuck in the studio with me."

Ryan fought to keep his jaw from dropping. Then again, based on previous conversations with Liz about her father's business, it made sense in a weird way.

However... "Even if you only took ID pictures, you still know how to aim a camera and focus and not cut off anyone's head."

Dan's laugh sounded forced. "I'd hope so." A moment later he raised his eyes. "I know my shots won't be as quality as yours or your friend's would have been, but I'd like the chance to try." His lips twisted into a semi-grin. "Even if I'll be praying extra hard for your boss to show up on time."

That made two of them, but in the meantime, they had a substitute photographer.

Ryan's shoulders relaxed, and he started to eat once more. Who knew that his appetite had only needed a project to focus on? He felt the twitch of a smile at his own pun.

Today might turn out just fine after all.

Three large bites later, Ryan shifted toward practicalities. "I'll set you up with my best camera. It will help with the quality of images—and then you can plan to take a bunch of photos before, during, and after the ceremony as well as at the reception. Like, take three times as many as you can possibly imagine. I'll personally edit and crop the photos later."

While hoping Dan captured something to work with.

And praying that Liz's slant toward collecting memories would overcome the potentially subpar photos of their wedding.

By the time their food was gone, the men had discussed a plan to waste a few more hours of the never-ending day by letting Dan practice with Ryan's camera.

As they sipped their coffees and waited for the check, Ryan turned the conversation to a nagging thought. "While I'm relieved that you're here, willing, and able to fill in for our missing photographer, I'm curious about something. If photography is not your passion, what would you really like to do?"

Dan stared over Ryan's shoulder for a minute as if weighing his words...or his thoughts. "I never had much of a chance to dream. I do like running a store with predictable routines. But I also enjoyed dabbling with woodworking after my heart surgery. I made a custom frame for a photo we got on our Maine trip, and it turned out very nicely."

"If you're talking about the picture hanging on the wall of your living room, I'd have to agree. The frame looked professionally done."

A glimmer of a smile flitted across Dan's face. "I might be interested in making custom frames for a photography studio. Then again, I'm not sure there's a big enough market in Wichita."

"If you're serious about possibly moving this direction, I could introduce you to several other photographers and gallery owners in the area." Ryan took a long swig of his coffee and contemplated the possibilities. "However, framing is probably something you could operate out of your garage rather than a storefront."

"True." A moment passed. "But if I opened a store to sell other picture-related things, my frames would be an added product in the inventory. Or...I could offer to turn people's photos into gifts. And specialize in all sorts of puzzles, along with the glue and frames, to turn those completed projects into something beautiful." Dan's voice gained energy and volume as more ideas began to flow.

Ryan bit back a smile. "I think you've just begun to dream."

"This trip has already brought up a lot to process. A new business is just one more thing to think about later." Dan grunted, but a genuine smile slipped through the facade. "But in the meantime, I've got a wedding to attend and try to photograph."

* * *

"All right, ladies, one more picture to help Liz remember what happened in the countdown blur before her wedding."

"Cheryl, don't make me regret handing you my camera." Liz glanced over her shoulder at her bridesmaids in their burgundy floor-length gowns as they sorted through the box of bouquets.

Ryan's sister just laughed and snapped the shutter anyway. "Like you didn't start documenting all this back at the salon with our hair still up in curlers."

"At least *now* we look half as stunning as the bride." Dani rolled her eyes.

"Good answer." Liz's attempt at a glare dissolved as her friends burst into another round of the happy giggles that had filled her day from their morning salon appointment through a late lunch at the hotel and on into the afternoon before they carpooled over to the church.

While Dani not so subtly suggested that Cheryl hide Liz's camera in her going-away suitcase sooner rather than later, Liz turned back to her mother.

The familiar actions behind the camera had kept her earlier nerves at bay. But now that she was in her gown in the bridal lounge at the church...with her mother helping adjust her veil atop her intricate up-do...

She could see their faces in the full-length mirror and distinctly remembered a different wedding where she'd been the photographer while hoping for this exact moment with her mother.

Liz fingered Grandma O'Neill's strand of pearls that her mother had brought and took a deep breath. "I'm so glad you're here with me."

"There's no place I'd rather be." Mom smoothed a piece of lace, then eyed their reflections. "You're a beautiful bride, and I'm so proud of the lovely woman you've become."

Blinking back tears and being only vaguely aware of the camera clicking behind her, Liz gathered her mother into a hug. "I love you, Mom."

A brisk knock on the door announced the arrival of the church's assigned wedding coordinator. "Good. You're all ready." The middle-aged woman glanced at her clipboard. "It's time to get your girls-only posed shots in the sanctuary."

"And you've made sure the guys are out of sight?" Liz turned to accept her bouquet from her matron-of-honor.

The woman quirked a half smile, as if she were used to pacifying nervous brides. "The only one left is the photographer."

Ah, yes. Ryan had told her that one of the other freelancers from work would be capturing their special day. Hopefully he could put some heart into his work and not treat it like another assignment.

Before she knew it, Liz was surrounded by bridesmaids—and even more giggles—as her friends helped with her train on the short walk to the sanctuary.

The room was even prettier than she'd imagined it could be since the florist had worked her magic. Especially at the front...where a single man in a suit waited with a camera in his hands.

A very familiar man.

Dad.

Liz gasped. Now here was someone who cared about both her and the event.

"Don't ruin your makeup." Mom's tone of voice made it clear that she'd known about this added surprise.

Her day couldn't get any better.

She wasn't the only one with tears when she finally reached his side.

His glistening eyes trailed over her from head to toe. "You're beautiful. Just like your mother." Dad's gaze drifted from her to her mother and then to the camera in his hands.

A camera which looked suspiciously like Ryan's Leica with the fast-action shutter.

"There was an unexpected delay with the real photographer, so Ryan asked if I could help out. I wish my pictures could do you justice. They'll be far from perfect—"

"No. They'll be perfect because I'll know that you took them."

And it was true...but that didn't mean she couldn't do her part by arranging the girls around her into the best poses she could imagine. The resulting relief on her dad's face made it even easier to smile. But when Dad snapped away from different angles and zoomed in and out, it was equally obvious that Ryan had been helping too, with tips as well as equipment.

All to make sure their day was perfect in every way.

Several dozen poses later, the wedding coordinator intruded and shooed them back to the bridal lounge so arriving guests could be seated. Then, precisely according to schedule, they were eventually directed to the foyer to line up for the processional.

After another hug, she relinquished her mother to be escorted down the aisle by the head usher. And then once again her dad was there—without the camera—to walk down with her.

He brushed a finger over her cheek. "My little girl has grown into a beautiful and extremely talented woman. Thank you for the honor of escorting you tonight." He grunted to clear his throat. "I may be giving you away, but I can't imagine a better man to give you to than Ryan."

"Me neither." Liz tugged a tissue out of the handle of her bouquet.

"I told him earlier today, but for what it's worth, you both have my full blessing."

"Thank you." Emotion blurred her eyes, and she carefully blotted away the tears before returning the damp tissue to its former hiding place.

Almost before she had regained control of her runaway joy, the music changed and the wedding coordinator began waving couples toward the front.

Liz linked arms with her dad and took her place at the back of the wedding party to await her turn.

But when she finally stepped through the doors into the sanctuary, the rest of the world faded into a blur as she focused on the grinning cowboy waiting at the altar.

For her.

The farther she moved down the aisle, the wider her smile grew…and the more intense his gaze became. Her heart caught in her throat.

The moment was everything she'd dreamed of.

Then, out of the corner of her eye, she caught the movement of another man kneeling in the aisle and wielding a camera like a pro. Because he was.

And her heart expanded even further at the sight of her boss and Ryan's mentor doing what he did best…for them.

World-class pictures.

Dad giving her away.

Mom on the front row, wiping happy tears from her eyes.

And Ryan.

Her handsome cowboy photographer met her near the front row, took her shaking hand in his strong grip, and led them to the altar, where the pastor began the ceremony to forever join their lives.

Only God could have orchestrated such a picture-perfect Christmas wedding.

Dear Reader,

You spoke. I listened. And hopefully you've enjoyed this continuation of Liz and Ryan's journey toward happily-ever-after.

Walking down the virtual aisle with one of my favorite fictional couples brought back a lot of memories from my own Christmas season wedding. Decorating the church was easy, and we added our own special touch with a giant tree at the reception for what else but the gifts! And in case you were wondering about a few of the other special details in the story: pecan shortbread snowballs are my favorite Christmas cookie, my youngest son makes me the best Hershey's Cocoa hot chocolate from scratch, I love working on big puzzles even if my family isn't as crazy about them, and I have indeed strung yards of popcorn as a decoration even if it was for my college dorm's decorating contest and the experience has yet to be repeated.

Writing a Christmas story was a lot of fun and helped distract me from the brutal heat back in July. Special thanks goes out to my editor extraordinaire Connie Troyer for moving all my commas and hyphens to where they belong. It's been a pleasure working together on the other books in The Wardrobe series as well.

If you think other readers would enjoy this story, please do me a huge favor and leave an honest review at Goodreads, Amazon, and other retailers. A review doesn't have to be more than a few words, but means so much to me!

Speaking of reviews, if you'd like to be a part of my official reviewer team with advance access to upcoming releases, you can email me at Candee@CandeeFick.com. Or if you'd rather just receive my monthly newsletter including information about upcoming releases, there's a sign-up spot available on my website at www.CandeeFick.com.

Thanks again for spending time with one of my books. Happy reading everyone!

CANDEE FICK

OTHER BOOKS BY CANDEE FICK

<u>Standalone</u>

Catch of a Lifetime

<u>The Wardrobe Series</u>

Dance Over Me
Focus On Love
Sing a New Song (available May 2019)
A Picture Perfect Christmas
Home For Christmas (coming November 2019)

<u>Within the Castle Gates</u>

Stepping Into the Light (coming January 2019)
To Win Her Heart (TBD)
The Lost Heir (TBD)
Finding Home (TBD)
Saving Grace (TBD)

<u>Non-Fiction</u>

The Author Toolbox: Practical Tools to Build a Book, a Platform,
a Business, and a Career
Pigskin Parables: Exploring Faith and Football
Pigskin Parables: Devotions from the Game of Football
Making Lemonade: Parents Transforming Special Needs
Devotions from the Garden: Inspiration for Life
Be Like a Tree: The Keys to a Fruitful Life

Read on for a peek at **Sing A New Song**, Book 3 of The
Wardrobe series followed by a preview of **Stepping Into the
Light**, Book 1 of the upcoming Within the Castle Gates series.

SING A NEW SONG

The Wardrobe series, Book 3
Releasing May 2019 from Bling! Romance

The pampered diva is about to meet her match.

Songbird Gloria Houghton has always needed to be the center of attention, but the spotlight has shifted. Seeking fame and a fresh start, she finds a new stage in Branson, Missouri...only to risk being replaced by a manipulative rival. If Gloria can't be the star, who is she?

Jack-of-all-trades Nick Sherwood is just one leaf on a vast family tree that includes restaurant chefs, hotel owners, and even the headline act at a family-owned theater. He's seen how fame can blind a person with jealousy and is more-than-content to stay in the background thank you very much. If only he wasn't so fascinated—and irritated—by the newest addition to the staff.

After a disaster of a first impression and financial difficulties land Gloria in the humblest of jobs—with Nick as her boss—it might be time for her to learn to sing a new song.

* * * * *

PROLOGUE

Friday, Mid-February
Gloria Houghton turned away from the list and faked a smile as her castmates congratulated her on another supporting role. She forced herself to take a deep breath, and then one more, as she squeezed through the crowd of actors outside the dressing rooms at The Wardrobe Dinner Theatre.

Yet the light-headed feeling remained. What would it take to regain her status as the leading lady? Then again, who was she kidding? She'd hoped for a bigger part this time, but she also knew that her surgically repaired knee couldn't take the beating. Oh, she could keep living on pain pills and ice packs and try not to limp through the season. The only other alternative was to tell the owners that she needed to take more time off—for what, physical therapy? Another surgery?

She should probably start with getting a second opinion from a medical professional before doing anything rash.

Near the back of the crowd, Dani stopped her progress. "Are you okay?"

A nod and another fake smile seemed to appease the actress. The same actress whose sparkling engagement ring only served as a glittering reminder that Gloria's grasp on love was as fleeting as her hold on the spotlight.

Gloria's stomach churned. It wasn't fair. She'd been part of the cast here first, but her position as the director's favorite had cracked and then crumbled. Former friends no longer followed her direction. And her on-again, off-again boyfriend seemed to want a new leading lady.

It was no wonder. Even she didn't like the bitter woman she had become.

And still Dani continued to be kind. Not to mention—as hard as it was to admit the truth—the other actress really had more talent, especially when it came to dancing.

Even Liz, the star of their current show, *Seven Brides for Seven Brothers,* had exceptional talent with a camera.

The only thing Gloria excelled at was singing.

The germ of an idea took root. She couldn't dance as much anymore, thanks to her lingering knee issues, but dancing had never been her favorite part to begin with. Acting wasn't that amazing either, since she'd been pretending her whole life to fill the role of the perfect daughter. For Gloria, it had always been about the music and the singing.

What if she found a stage and a show where all they did was sing ... with maybe a little bit of choreography, but nothing as taxing as the extended tap-dancing numbers of her current job?

She turned away from the others crowded around the dressing rooms and looked for a quiet place to think as the idea grew. Was it possible to still be a part of the "glitz and glamour" of show business but only do what she enjoyed most?

As she passed the wings, she spotted Liz standing in the middle of the dimly lit stage. Beyond the closed curtain, several hundred people were finishing their meals and making their intermission dessert selections. The cast members scheduled to wait tables tonight would be hustling to refill drinks, while back near the dressing rooms others put the finishing touches on their stage makeup, double-checked costumes, or rehashed the casting decisions for the next production.

Next weekend Liz would be gone, pursuing a new chapter in her life. And Gloria would fill her shoes in the role of Milly, the first bride in the list of *Seven Brides for Seven Brothers*. For four beautiful weekends, the bright lights would blind her to the audience as she lost herself in a fictional world through singing and dancing.

And then the spotlight would shift to a new star in the next play.

Gloria shook her head and moved toward Liz. "Saying goodbye or regretting your decision?"

"No regrets." Liz turned to face her with a wistful smile on her face. "I'm glad you have the chance to take a lead role again, even if it's only for a few weeks."

Gloria quirked an eyebrow. "So you knew about that joke of a cast list?"

"No." Liz glanced toward the dressing rooms. "I didn't look since I wouldn't be here, but I assume you're not happy."

"That's putting it mildly." Gloria blew out a breath. "They put Renee and Sarah in the top two female roles and I'm stuck in the ensemble again. While Evan's already flirting with his new costar. Ever since I hurt my knee, nothing's gone my way around here." A clumsy fall in her kitchen had torn her knee and ripped the starring role from her grasp, leaving behind the pain of dashed dreams and the nagging fear that she would never regain the spotlight.

"Nothing?" Liz gestured to the stage around them. "You're about to be Milly."

"A lot of good that will do, because the future isn't looking so bright."

"Some things are more important than the spotlight."

"Well, I guess I haven't found them yet." Gloria looked around the stage area. Had it always been so small? "And I'm not sure I'll ever find them here."

Maybe it was time for her to say goodbye to musical theater too and focus on singing instead.

"I hope you find what you're looking for." Liz smiled and then drifted away toward one of the wings, leaving Gloria alone at center stage.

Her voice could be her magic ticket to the future. But where?

She didn't necessarily want a solo act, so those television audition shows to find the next voice were out of the question. And while actresses flocked to Hollywood or New York City, most singers usually ended up in Nashville—only to get lost in the crowd of hopefuls.

Gloria slowly paced the polished boards of the stage. Where could she get in the door and meet musical people who could take her places? She needed to find an abundance of shows where lots of tourists came. Vegas? No way. She shuddered at the thoughts of drunk tourists, the skimpy costumes to satisfy the gamblers, and the "What Happens in Vegas Stays in Vegas" slogan.

Even she had personal standards. But where else should she go?

Dani would tell her to pray about it. Liz too. For all the good praying would do.

But, God, if You even exist, please give me a stage.

Four hours later, she sprawled on the couch of her shared apartment with an ice pack on her throbbing knee and a late-night talk show on the television screen. The host finished his monologue, then introduced a new performing group with an act fresh from the strip in Branson, Missouri.

They had shows there?

Her fingers flew across the screen of her phone, revealing a row of theaters where dozens of musical variety shows catered to thousands of tourists. And judging by the list of names, the town had a reputation for quality music, even if it slanted toward country.

If she made her name known there, who knew where she could end up?

Yes, the time had come for a change of scenery. She'd stick it out for one more show, but come spring she'd reign over a new stage and be one step closer to her dreams.

* * * * *

Want to read more of *Sing a New Song*?
Find all the details (including buying links once available) on
my website at www.CandeeFick.com.

STEPPING INTO THE LIGHT

Within the Castle Gates series, Book 1
Releasing January 2019

Sometimes the most heroic live in plain sight.

Tragedy stalks the Gunn castle, most recently when the heir to the Gunn chiefdom died leaving their land vulnerable to attack. But security has come in the promise of a marriage alliance with Clan Sinclair, their powerful neighbors to the north.

The search is on to gather the eligible maidens...except mysterious accidents befall all who join the laird's widow at the castle. Meanwhile, messengers have been spotted along their southern border and Clan Sinclair may be walking into a trap.

With war looming and a madwoman in their midst, the only hope for a peaceful future may lie in the hands of a disfigured Gunn recluse and the overlooked second son of Clan Sinclair.

* * * * *

PROLOGUE

1412 ~ Scottish Highlands
Alone at last, Moira Gunn collapsed to her knees in the middle of the glade.

Chest heaving from her dash away from the castle, she sat back on her heels and inhaled the pine-scented air. Today it might take more than her favorite hideaway to restore her peace.

She dried her tears with the edge of the Gunn clan's woolen plaid draped around her slight frame, then studied her surroundings.

Ears keen to a rustling in the nearby underbrush, her breath caught in her throat. Her heart pounded as the peace around her shattered.

A flash of red through the branches confirmed her worst fears moments before Devlin, the captain of Isla's personal guard pushed through the undergrowth into the clearing. The laird's wife insisted on the unique shirt color as proof of their authority, except it only made the ruffians easier to spot...and avoid.

Until today.

"Look who I found outside the castle gates." Devlin sneered from a stone's toss away. "Thought ye could sneak out, did ye?"

Mayhap there was naught to fear but another tongue-lashing. Still, Moira slowly eased to her feet, prepared to bluff her way out of the danger prickling the back of her neck.

Either that or run.

Except even with scattered thickets and patches of brambles, the stretch of forest between the castle wall and the nearby ravine wouldna hide her for long.

Devlin took a step closer. "Lady Isla sent ye to the kitchens for a reason."

'Twas punishment for ruining her gown as they broke their fast that morn, except 'twasna her fault. Ilsa's spoiled son Roan had smeared the fruit tart onto her skirt, then stood silently by—and smirking—whilst Moira shouldered the blame.

"But I didna…" Her voice trailed off. Her father's new wife never believed her and lately she'd spent more time away from her family than with them.

"Ye were sent to prepare the meal for yer clan." Devlin crossed bulging arms across his chest, an angry scowl marring his face.

Moira side-stepped a patch of multi-colored flowers to put more distance between them.

She might have been happy helping in the kitchens, but the cook had complained she was underfoot and didna belong there.

Didna seem she belonged anywhere.

Especially by her father's side.

A sob caught in her throat. The whole clan had been abuzz for days with speculation about their laird's mysterious illness until she simply couldn't face another moment of the gossip feeding her fears.

What would she do if he died? Who would protect her then?

Members of their clan came to offer their herbal cures and pay their respects to their laird. Yet she wasna even allowed to sing for him like she had many times before.

Still, a lass should be allowed to greet her father on her birthday, especially her thirteenth when she officially moved from bairn to maiden.

She fingered the jeweled brooch hanging from a leather cord around her neck. Her gift three years ago while her mother was still alive.

Today held no gifts, only a heavy cloud.

The verra reason she'd sought the neglected side gate in the curtain wall and slipped away to rail at the injustice her life had become.

When Father Tomas returned from the Sinclair holding, she would ask him why good people died. And why God seemed so far away.

A twig snapped.

Too late, Moira realized she'd gotten distracted by her musings.

In three quick steps, Devlin reached her side and a hand snaked out to wrap around the plaited hair hanging down her back.

"Don't ya ken? It be dangerous for a lass to be alone in the woods."

Panic coursed through her veins and she struggled against the tightening grip that anchored her in place. "Let me go. My da will hear of this and—"

"He won't be causing any more trouble. And neither will ye." He laughed, his foul breath hot on her face. "And ye won't be needin' this anymore." A vicious jerk later and her precious heirloom had been ripped away.

The burning fire around her throat mirrored the agonizing void in her heart. "My mother's brooch—"

"Not anymore."

A moment later, he waved his dagger before her eyes.

Icy dread settled in her stomach at the sight of the wickedly sharp blade.

"There's only room for one pretty lady at the keep."

"I'm just a lass." She struggled to break free of his hold.

Was he here out of some sort of misguided loyalty? Or jealousy on behalf of his mistress?

Heaven help her if he meant to scar her for life.

A brutal yank on her hair sent her spinning. He released her for an instant, but before she could gather her wits, she found herself facing the clearing but trapped against his body. Anchored in place by a meaty hand on her forehead.

"Yer the one he's calling for in his fevered sleep." His dagger danced before her eyes. "All he can say is 'Mor.' "

Her heard ached at the drawn-out—cruel—imitation of a suffering man's delirium. Then stopped as recognition dawned.

"Mor. Mor." The traitorous guard's mocking laughter rang out through the clearing as cold metal trailed down her cheek.

Moira's knees weakened at the sound of her dear mother's name. The mother who'd died in childbirth followed a few days later by her infant son. Would they all soon be reunited in the hereafter?

"Well, no more." The blade came to rest beneath her chin.

Lightheaded with fear, her knees buckled and she found herself falling, slipping from his grasp even as the prick of the blade pierced her neck, then sliced up the side of her face with agonizing heat.

Her scream was silenced by harsh reality. With the knife at her throat, he had truly meant to kill her.

Only God could help her now.

A surge of unexpected strength sent her rolling to her right, then scrambling to her feet before running blindly into the woods. The crashing of feet behind her drove her further from the safety of home and toward the distant rush of water as she darted one way and then the other around trees.

Despite the hand pressed against her face, every step jarred the injury, sending more blood trickling through her fingers and down her arm.

She rounded a cluster of tall bushes, then glanced back over her shoulder. He gained on her, a look of fury twisting his features and the bloody dagger still in his hand.

Suddenly, the ground fell away, leaving her to tumble down the rock-strewn wall of the ravine. After a final rolling catapult off a large boulder, she landed on her back near the creek. Gasping like a fish on land, she fought to draw air into her lungs.

Above her came a bellow of outrage, reminding her to stay quiet—and motionless—in case he couldn't already see her broken body at the bottom of the ravine.

A moment later, the vice-like grip around her chest eased enough for her to breathe again. Just in time for every bruise and scrape acquired during her fall to raise their voices in protest, joining the pulsing agony from her face.

Risking detection as Devlin stomped overhead, she lifted weak hands to hold the slashed flesh together, then bit back a whimper at the renewed throbbing that brought tears to her eyes.

"When I find ye, ye'll wish ye were already dead."

Death might be welcome considering the misery of the moment. Then again, her father had always told her to be a brave lass because Gunns never quit.

A deep growl in the brush above her 'twas followed by a howl that sent chills up her already-battered spine. A wolf. Somehow, either the man's actions or the scent of her blood had attracted the attention of the beast.

The guard's war cry split through the air and soon the sounds of battle between man and beast faded further away.

Thank Heaven for the distraction, but the rest of the pack might be nearby.

Still dizzy from her fall, Moira eyed a nearby cluster of purple-hued bell heather. A half hour past, she would have relished the simple beauty of the flowering blooms and soaked in the happy twittering of lapwings in the branches overhead.

Yet now, she could already tell her body weakened from the loss of blood. If she didna wish to die when Devlin returned, she must get away.

Now.

Somehow, she staggered to her feet and stumbled along the creek bed toward the loch.

Her last memory was of coming upon an elderly man with a wooden cart.

* * * * *

Want to read more of *Stepping Into the Light*?
Find all the details (including buying links once available) on my website at www.CandeeFick.com.

ABOUT THE AUTHOR

Candee Fick is a romance editor for a small Christian press and a multi-published award-winning author. She is the wife of a high school football coach and the mother of three children, including a daughter with a rare genetic syndrome. When not busy editing or writing, she can be found cheering on the home team at sporting events, exploring the great Colorado outdoors, indulging in dark chocolate, and savoring happily-ever-after endings through a good book.

In addition to writing clean faith-based romance novels and inspirational non-fiction, Candee coaches other authors with their marketing plans and offers content editing to aspiring novelists. She is a member of both American Christian Fiction Writers (ACFW) and the Christian Proofreaders and Editors Network. Her fiction has semi-finaled, finaled, and won the ACFW Genesis Contest and Selah Awards.